MONSTROUS TALES – VOLUME 1
A Horror Anthology of
Longer Stories For A Satisfying Read

I0557997

Edited by Dorothy Davies

MONSTROUS TALES – VOLUME 1
A Horror Anthology of
Longer Stories For A Satisfying Read

GRAVESTONE PRESS

CONTENTS

CONTENTS

Visiting Granddad
SJ Townend

Despite the doctor telling him to cut back on the fried food, the toffees, the protein, if Granddad was cooking himself dinner, he was cooking something he damn well liked. Tonight it was greasy and meaty. *Bah humbug to the Vegan Youth and the 'meat is murder' brigade.* He'd been a young boy in the fifties when meat was a privilege, meat had been a luxury, so no doctor was going to tell him what he could and couldn't eat.

He put his teeth in a bourbon glass next to his plate, acrylic smiling at porcelain and sat down next to Grandma to start his supper.

Knock, knock, knock.

The door.

He chose to ignore it.

He pierced the ox tongue with his fork, anchoring it to the face of the plate and drew his favourite steak knife back and forth and back and forth until a morsel large enough to enjoy but small enough for toothless mastication hung speared on the end of his fork. He chomped on the soft gobbet, bashing and smacking it against his gums, eyes closed and mouth opened and let out an audible moan of delight as the blood in the meat released and trickled into his palette. The knock at the door was repeated.

Damn them, coming now. We've just sat down to eat, he thought. With a bony finger, he tapped Grandma on her shoulder. She was a little hard of hearing, silly old mare. Chair legs scraped on the cold stone floor as she rose from her place at the table.

"Hi. Sorry, I thought you would've already eaten." It was their daughter Lisa and grandson Billy. Granddad wiped a rivulet of crimson from his jaw as Grandma ushered the pair in. With a spindly arm and no words but a grumble, he gestured at the sofa—all leather and sticky with the heat of the evening—and the boy sat down. Granddad continued with his food.

"It smells like liver and onions in here, Grandma. Are you eating *offal* again—?" Lisa stopped mid-sentence as her father threw her a look which hit like a cold hand, a physical strike from a time long ago when it had been acceptable to spank.

"No, dear, I've gone for a low-fat quiche," said Grandma.

"Thanks for having Billy." Lisa was on her way to work. "Perhaps you could teach him how to play chess or show him Granddad's old fishing rods?" She'd managed to secure a second job at the drive-through, serving coffee to juggernaut drivers and cops. She'd needed the additional income since the kid's father had up and left.

"I'll be here at eight thirty tomorrow morning to pick him up."

8

Grandma nodded and smiled at her daughter. Lisa noted how much happier Grandma seemed these days; she had quite the metaphorical spring in her hobbled step.

"Just make sure you're no later than eight thirty tomorrow," Granddad hissed, not even looking up from his meal. "I've treatment at nine."

With a lean stare, he looked at the boy, held his glare a little longer than the boy found comfortable, then returned his attention to his dish. Billy looked at his mother and wondered if she had caught Granddad's displeased look too.

"Everything Billy needs is in his bag. Just remind him to brush his teeth before bed, if you could."

The old man's eyes flicked to his own teeth in the glass and back again to the boy. Billy's eyes were drawn to the ticking sound coming from the mantelpiece. In his home, the mantelpiece was crowded with photographs of him and his mother, ornaments, paintings and pieces he had crafted at school. Here, the mantelpiece was bare. Barren apart from a heavy, antique vase, a blanket of dust and an eerie bronze carriage clock that looked older than Grandma and older still than Granddad.

"Too-da-loo," said Grandma, as Lisa, swept up in the struggle of motherhood and work and the ever pressing hand of punctuality, hugged her son and left.

Billy pulled a book from his bag. He knew not to disturb his grandfather whilst Grandma pottered in the kitchen. He had brought plenty of books to read—on Sauropoda and the Jurassic era—so he could hide behind the pages, two hundred and four million years away, until he was sent to bed, until his mother picked him up in the morning.

This was the second time his mother had left him there overnight since they had moved back from the other side of the country to her home town, after the messy divorce. The first time had been no fun at all, despite Grandma playing draughts with him and showing him how to knit. Billy was a good boy and knew his mother needed the money, so he had quietly got in the car again to stay the night with his grandparents.

He really just wanted to run and jump and play as he was an active boy, full of beans, but he knew his grandparents would not want to do any of those things. Granddad was old and Granddad was also unwell—he'd been in and out of hospital for months, Mother said he was in need of a long rest—and Grandma walked with a cane. Mother had told Billy about Granddad needing 'die-ali-sis'. His body couldn't keep his blood clean. His body had given up. Mother had explained about the machine which helped to keep him going. He'd asked his mother to explain what she'd meant, but she just muttered something about kidneys. Was it why Granddad ate so much bloody food, organ meat, he pondered? Granddad certainly had the diet of a carnivorous dinosaur, but Billy thought he looked more like a grey tortoise when he chewed bluntly on his meat.

***

Billy hated kidneys. Steak and kidney pie, kidney bean chilli: his two least favourite meals. He was glad that Grandma catered for him and Granddad never offered to cook.

He'd seen the inside of the old man's fridge. He kept a separate one out in the garage, additional to Grandma's one in the kitchen. Granddad made him look in his garage fridge the last time he'd stayed over, after he'd asked Grandma for more dessert: tripe and sweetmeats with nothing sweet about them, black pudding galore—not a vegetable or fruit in sight. "Look here, boy. Stop hassling your Grandma for sweets. You need more protein in your diet to keep you healthy and strong. Sweets will rot your teeth," Granddad had said to the child. After showing him his fridge, Granddad grabbed the boy, opened his tortoise jaw and showed the boy his red raw gums as close as he could without placing the child's nose inside his mouth. Billy recalled that his breath had stunk, bitter like decaying flesh and cloying like funeral flowers.

The only redeeming feature of Granddad's diet, as far as Billy was concerned, was the jar of toffees he'd spotted on his first visit. It sat on the top shelf in the lounge, full to the brim last week, silently shouting promises of sugary licks all evening to the

11

boy's rumbling stomach. Granddad hadn't offered him one, though, and the boy had been too scared to ask. He couldn't have reached the jar even if he had dared to try, but alas, he could see it was now empty. Sucked dry, no doubt, by the greedy old man.

***

After Granddad had eaten, he popped his teeth back in and sat in his chair by the fire to work on a crossword. Sometimes he stared at the child with an intimidating expression: a smidgen of contempt, a scornful face of disdain. At other times, he stared at Billy with the same look that he held each supper, whilst carving the pieces up small enough for his palate to cope with: a hankering, a thirst, an impatience.

Billy didn't like it when Granddad looked at him and liked it even less when Granddad asked questions, so Billy bided his time whilst his Grandmother darned old stockings. He hid all evening behind his book until he was sent off to bed.

The following morning, Lisa came to collect her son. She smiled with all her face and kissed Billy on the cheek. "See you Friday then—if you're still okay to have him again?"

"Sure, would love that," Grandma replied, smiling with her full face too, like a sunny Saturday.

12

"We'll have him," Granddad whispered, smiling with only his pallid lips as Lisa waved goodbye.

Then Granddad went out to the garage after checking on his meat supply, folded himself into his car and headed to the hospital.

THRICE A WEEK. FOUR HOURS A POP. PUNCTURED. TUBES. ALL HOOKED UP. GOODBYE TOXIC WASTE. SIT. SIT. SIT. BLOOD COME OUT. BLOOD GO IN. CLEAN AGAIN. CLEAN AGAIN. CUP OF TEA. TICK TOCK, HOME TIME.

***

That Friday, Billy was dropped off at his grandparent's again and immediately burrowed into his book as Granddad dined on slivers of brain dripping in a red-brown gravy sauce. The house smelt like the old fox's body Billy found under the decking in the basement of his old home, awash with maggots, a space where an eye once existed. Billy missed his old house. The boy felt his stomach flip with the sensation of erupting vomit as the old man sliced and chomped on piece after piece of congealed meat. As he watched, he thought about the fox. With fearful eyes poking over the top of his book, Billy couldn't help but look at the glass with the teeth in it and the congealed mess on the

13

old man's plate whilst Granddad focused solely on his meal.

At nine, Billy was sent to the spare room and he was glad to go. His Grandma kissed him on the forehead and read him a story, then he got into bed and pulled the itchy sheet up to under his chin, to make sure there were no gaps around the edges for things of the night to get in.

Turbulent dreams of Cyclops-fox corpses and cutlery teasing and tearing at animal flesh followed and, as he turned over mid-nightmare, he abruptly awoke, releasing a loud scream of pain. He flicked on the dusty lamp beside the bed and shrieked again at the red sight before and around him.

Blood.

A wound in his side, leaking vermillion liquid onto the crumpled bed linen, gleaming in the only light of the night, yelled for his attention. He pressed his hands against his flank, probing for the source of his injury to find a slice of glass, triangular, sharp like a dinosaur tooth, pressing in to his flesh and as he wriggled to try and see the damage it'd done, he sliced himself again. The boy jumped up and out of his bed and switched on the ceiling light. A buttery glow revealed a sea of shards, mostly in his bed, from where a smashed glass had shared itself around. And there, by the side of his pillow, like a fish out of water and dead, his grandfather's teeth sat.

The boy stemmed the flow of blood from ribboning further down his side with tissues, and then, in the hallway he saw his Grandfather.

"Good Lord, boy. What's all the noise about—are you trying to wake the neighbours?"

"Granddad— "

The boy's pulse quickened at the sight of the old man stood there, dressed still in his day clothes, minus his teeth. Billy's heart pealed for his mother.

"What are you doing, Boy? Let go of the tissue. You need to let it bleed."

"B... bleed?" he stammered. "I think I need to make it stop, that's what Mother would say."

Granddad let out a hiss, shook his head at the boy and then shook his head again at Grandma as she approached—slowly, hobbling—before trundling back down the hallway.

Grandma, cane in hand, shuffled into the boy's room, her eyes widening at the sight of the smashed glass.

"Grandma... Grandma... I'm hurt," the boy said and carefully tiptoed towards her, pointing at his side.

His Grandma wrapped an arm around the boy, comforting him as he cried. "There's nothing there boy, nothing. You're fine. Your eyes are playing tricks on you, like my ears fool me in the silence of the night. Now stop all this kerfuffle. Help me clear up this mess."

On hands and knees, the old woman and the boy slowly collected the shards, wrapped them up in newspaper and disposed of them in the bin. She tucked him up in fresh sheets and kissed him on the forehead before leaving him alone with only the light of the bedside lamp for company. Until only moments after the boy's heart rate had dropped to a level at which the call of sleep could be heard, Granddad returned.

"What in heaven's name are you doing with my teeth, boy?" his grandfather sneered. "Your mother would be furious to hear how you've been meddling. If she was to catch wind of any of this, my God, boy, she'd skin you raw. That woman has enough on her plate."

With that, the old man crouched and snatched his teeth from where they'd fallen under the bed.

Billy sat shivering and dabbing at imagined blood until his mother came to collect him the next day.

In the morning, an exhausted Billy left with his mother. Grandma prepared lunch and Granddad went again to Nephrology.

SIT. SIT. SIT. BLOOD COME OUT. BLOOD GO IN. CLEAN AGAIN. CLEAN AGAIN. TICK TOCK, HOME TIME.

***

The following week, Billy had not wanted to stay at his grandparents. He'd pleaded with his mother to let him stay with her, but she told him he needed to

16

go, he didn't have a choice and, in fact, he needed to spend a little longer there this time—she would be dropping him off after lunch.

Reluctantly, the boy went. In the car, on the way over, Lisa told Billy that she'd arranged for Grandma to take him swimming. She suggested, perhaps, that he could impress her by showing her how well he jumped a bomb into the pool. Billy wasn't convinced. He wasn't the strongest swimmer, in fact he still liked to stay in the shallow end, as his young arms and legs tired quickly when pushing and treading the water. He did enjoy swimming, though. He wanted to make his mother happy and he hadn't been to the pool in this neck of the woods, so he agreed to go.

"Be a good boy," Lisa said, kissing her son on the forehead and waving at him from her car as he walked up the pathway and knocking hesitantly on the front door.

Grandma let the boy in.

"I'll be back same time, in the morning," shouted Lisa from the driver's seat. "Trunks and towel are in his bag."

Grandma scurried to the kitchen to finish off her ironing. Granddad said nothing to the boy; just took his hand and led him out to the garage to show him more meat before helping him into the car.

Billy had never seen such a physique before. Grandma looked as Grandmas do, crumpled, vaguely transparent, spilling out from a swimsuit from a different era, but Granddad, well, he looked like a skeletal apparition of what the boy had imagined as he exited the changing rooms, towel bundled under his armpit. White skin suckered and sagging down over his xylophone birdcage of ribs, blue-green veins clinging to and winding up the backs of his legs like parasitic vines choking silver birch saplings. Granddad was shivering before he'd even entered the water. The boy couldn't help looking at the plastic tubing protruding from the old man's arm, a tiny red tap attached to its end, like a place one could fix a hosepipe to. He wanted to ask what the pipe work was for—was his grandfather a cyborg, an inflatable toy, a maple syrup tree? But he didn't dare.

The old man sighed with the weight of the world on his shoulders and his spine hunched in this way too. He looked at the rectangular pool of water full of children splashing, having fun, people on lunch breaks, swimming up and down, circumventing the puerile mayhem, ants at a picnic; incessant, relentless, with their endless lengths. Stood waist high in the cold water, Granddad asked himself: would he rather be sat at dialysis?

No, this is just a means to an end.

"Look, boy, you know I'm not well. And your Grandma, well, she can't swim far at all, look at her. You can almost see the arthritis rotting and spilling out of her crick-crack knees. And I can't get my port arm wet, so thus, I can't really swim, either. We'll just stand here and watch."

"I understand, Granddad," the boy replied as his Grandma nattered to a friend she'd spotted from rummy club. Billy tried not to look at the old man's frail body, the port in his arm, the toothless mouth, the tracing paper skin.

"But your mother wants you to impress us, me in particular I expect. She's always felt sad you and I haven't ever bonded. I'm sure she'd want you to show me... just how good you are at diving. Your mother needs you to try a little harder with the bonding. Seems all one way, so far."

"I don't think she said diving," the boy trembled, not with the cold of the water.

"Hush now, boy. Contradict me again; you'll get a mouth like mine." Granddad's words came out quietly but with the force of smoke venting from a crematory flue.

The boy's heart started to pound like a race horse's. All his blood sank to his toes. Did his grandfather just threaten to knock out his teeth?

"Diving, boy. Your mother clearly stated you could dive. Up there, from the springboard."

Granddad raised his gnarly arm and pointed to the white plank, oscillating up and down, wafting outwards a scent of chlorine and fear. Billy stared up as a child much older than him jumped from it, up, up, into the air and down, down, into the water, elegant like a bird with its eye on a plump sea fish.

He looked over at Grandma. She was mid-story and his mother had taught him it's rude to interrupt. "I—"

"Get up those steps, now, Boy. Dive for me," the old man hissed, a venomous snake spitting poisoned words into only the boy's ears.

The quivering boy felt frozen to the spot but Granddad reached under the water, pinched the skin where no scar from the glass was to be found and twisted it hard and firm.

The boy squealed, his heart a wave-crest of stallions bucking and galloping and pushed his way through the water to the steps. He climbed out and found his feet taking him up the ladder. He walked slowly to the cusp of the board, his ears a-wash with the noise of children screaming and the pounding of his own blood thrumming through veins by his ears. He edged to the tip of the diving board and looked down below. All the while, he could feel the eyes of his Grandfather picking like arrows into his naked torso. He felt sick with fear. He'd never been so high up before, let alone over a large body of water filled with people's scalps and shoulders. Billy had no idea what he was doing but was pretty sure he wouldn't be able to touch the bottom of the deep end. Surely Granddad wouldn't make him do something unsafe? He took a big breath and held it, swan-necked his arms out in front like he'd seen Olympic divers do on television and stepped off of the end.

He fell like a rock and hit the water hard with a bang. Grandma looked up and screamed, her voice lost amongst the reverberating sounds of the crowded pool. Granddad watched, smirking.

Stupid boy. Stupid, healthy boy.

The boy rose up to the surface, coughing and spluttering and crying. Grandma had seen and had started to wade through the water. She shouted, "Billy, Billy, please... help him," to no avail. He couldn't touch the bottom; he hadn't even come close to the bottom on the first crash into the water. He couldn't reach the side and he couldn't get enough air in as his head came up to the surface. His arms flayed above his head as his feet got tangled in the depths and not a soul seemed alarmed, other than his Grandma who was still slowly paddling towards a lifeguard. He dropped again into the water, his head going under again too.

This was a time of nightmares.

Gruesome visions flashed by, sea monsters, eyeless foxes, bad mer-people hiding behind waves of shards of glass, teeth, something wet sitting on his chest. He kicked his legs harder and harder to try and reach the surface again. The water was winning. The boy was sinking.

Granddad was smiling.

A whistle blew—Grandma had made it to the lifeguard—swimmers moved away from the struggling boy, a biblical parting of the ocean ensued as a lifeguard threw a red float on a rope in toward Billy. He tried to reach it and kicked with all his might but it seemed to be drifting further and further away.

A lady shouted, "I'll get him," to the life guard who was taking off his trainers on the side of the pool.

The woman swam, lifted Billy up and guided him like an angel to the float and the lifeguard yanked the boy to the side. He was lifted out of the water. A metallic sheet was wrapped around his shoulders and he became a failed superhero. He shuddered and shivered as he became a wrap of cold meat prepared for the fridge.

Grandma hugged the wet, crying boy tightly. "Oh, Billy, if only your Gramps had been well, there, down at the deep end, he'd have saved you. He used to be such a strong swimmer. I'm sorry, love."

Everybody cheered the lifeguard and the lady who helped to save him. The swimmers all clapped with joy.

Except for Granddad.

He made his way over and said, "I couldn't reach you. I'm ill, you see. I can't get my port wet." He gestured at his arm, smiling politely at the lifeguard, but only with his lips.

They dressed, left the swimming venue and made the journey home. The boy went straight to the spare room and closed the door behind him. He got under the sheets, pulled them up tight round his neck and started to cry harder than he'd ever cried before.

"Granddad, why did you make me do it?" He was talking to himself. He was crying for his mother. He was wishing the clock on the mantelpiece would tick a little faster and it could be tomorrow so he could go home. Granddad stood outside the door, listening.

"You're no use to me like this," the old man said under his breath before heading out to the garage to take out a pair of lamb's kidneys from the fridge which he would sear gently on either side and sauté with a little garlic for his supper.

***

The next day, Lisa came to collect the boy and told Grandma how exhausted she was.

"I wouldn't know what to do without you," she said as her son clung onto his mother with relief. "I don't know how we'd cope." A tear fell from her eye as she smiled with her lips and also with her whole face. Billy thought her smile felt like sunshine after the rain. The old man grunted whilst Grandma waved them off and then he headed off himself for his treatment.

SIT. SIT. SIT. BLOOD COME OUT. BLOOD GO IN. CLEAN AGAIN. CLEAN AGAIN. TICK TOCK, HOME TIME.

***

Billy felt a strong hatred for his grandfather growing in the pit of his belly, but he loved his Grandma. She was always smiling and he couldn't bear to see his mother sad. So, the following week, he found himself being marched to his grandparent's front door step again, dropped off with a bag of books and a heart full of fear.

"Want some meat, boy?" Granddad offered the boy a slice of blue steak. Billy declined without words, shaking his head from behind the shield of his hardback book. He stared at the clock on the mantel piece. Just half an hour more until bed time. He'd packed a torch in his bag, and this time, he'd also packed a knife from his mother's cutlery drawer. He went to the room allocated to him, he slid the knife under the pillow and sat on the corner of the bed, torch in hand, reading to keep himself awake. His eyes felt heavy and weighted and, try as he might, at around 2am he couldn't fight sleep's call any longer.

***

He didn't hear the footsteps, or the creaking of the door, it was the feeling of the velvet swathed cushion on his face that woke him as Granddad peered down at the boy with crazed, marbled eyes and breath that stank of fox shit and flesh. The boy squirmed and struggled, fearing for his life again, as the old man pushed down with all the weight of his decrepit body. Billy tossed and turned in a fit of fear. The old man grimaced and sneered.

The boy slipped his hand under the pillow and pulled out his knife. The old man laughed as a slice of light from the streetlamp outside nosed in through a slit in the curtains and reflected off the curved steel piece.

"Butter knife, hey, Boy?" he spluttered from his aged throat. "You really are a fool."

He knocked the knife clean from the boy's hand.

"You little bastard. Come on, just give them to me. You've got more than enough to spare. Die, you little shit."

The boy panicked, his brain running short of oxygen, but as the old man pushed down a little harder on Billy's face, all four eyes just a few inches from each other, the boy drew his foot up and out from under the weight of the itchy sheets and kicked the old man between the legs. He recoiled in pain, throwing the pillow to the floor, clutching his crotch with both hands.

Billy got up, ran to the door of the bedroom and burst straight out of the house, up the path, up and up to the end of the street, bare feet shouting out in pain from the sharpness of the pavement.

The boy ran and ran and pounded the pavements under the blanket blackness of a sombre night, the thick sky pierced only by bubbles of amber light at the top of each streetlamp; orbs of buttery haze, hellish midnight dandelions in seed.

He made it to the café where he crept, crying with sore feet, up to the building. His throat was burning from the marathon he'd just completed. He sat and watched his mother through the window.

She looked as sad and tired as he felt. She too was run off her feet, waiting on large, angry truckers. After catching his breath, the boy sat and cried some more and hugged his knees in tightly. He waited there, hidden, until the end of her shift and then ran up to her as she came out.

"Billy? Billy!" she screamed. "What on earth are you doing here?" He wanted to tell her what Granddad had done, but couldn't, because he knew how much her job meant, even though she'd looked so unhappy through the cafe window. The adult world made no sense at all to Billy.

She shepherded the boy into her car and gave him tissues to wipe the sleep and tears from his eyes until he felt safe again. He fell asleep on the drive home.

In the morning, he told his mother he'd had a nightmare and hadn't wanted to wake Grandma up because she was exhausted from all the swimming. She explained to him that he must never behave like that again and he promised, with a painful squeezing feeling in his chest, that he wouldn't.

Lisa called Grandma. She passed the phone over to her son so that he could apologise to her, but as Billy placed his ear to the receiver, he felt a wet, warm lick, smelt the old fox's scent and heard his Granddad's voice down the line.

"You're spoilt, boy. You're ruining your mother's life, stop causing all this trouble." After that, the dial tone began and Billy passed the phone back to his mother, his face as pale as a sheet. He said nothing for the rest of the day.

Granddad then got in his car and headed off for his final treatment.

SIT. SIT. SIT. BLOOD COME OUT. BLOOD GO IN. CLEAN AGAIN. CLEAN AGAIN. TICK TOCK, HOME TIME.

***

"The kidney is often the first organ to fail, if you're blessed enough to reach old age," the consultant had said after Granddad's first round of dialysis. The old man had sucked a sharp whistle of air in through the gap in his false teeth in response to the doctor's useless words.

"I'm afraid the only permanent solution would be a fresh young kidney plumbed into your failing urinary system." The old man had sighed; borrowed time. Borrowed time. Borrowed kidneys. Each word had felt like a coffin nail slamming into his chest.

***

The next time Lisa tried to take Billy to his grandparents' house, he feigned a stomach ache, a headache, a sore throat, but she checked him and he seemed okay to her. She let Grandma know to call her straight away if he started to show serious symptoms. The boy pleaded and pleaded with her not to leave him there, but she said she simply needed to get to work, even though she had tears in her eyes too.

He tried to tell himself he was mistaken, that Granddad couldn't possibly be so mean. Perhaps he was just imagining it all, like the fox that kept visiting him in his dreams, with its missing eye, its gangrenous limbs, its splaying entrails.

Before she got into her car to leave, Lisa pulled out a bag of toffees and passed them to Billy's Grandma.

"Here. Share these over a bedtime story. I'm so sorry about his behaviour. I've made him promise it won't happen again."

"You'll be a good boy for your grandmother, for your mother, lad, won't you?" Granddad said through fake teeth and fake smile as Lisa waved goodbye. Then Grandma went inside and the old man pulled Billy back into the house, locked the door behind them and pushed the child onto the sofa. Grandma went upstairs to make up a fresh bed for her grandson.

"I only put up with you up because you have something I need and you and I both know what that is," the old man hissed through furred, whiskered lips, with sour breath, with a swoosh of his ginger tail dipped in cream, as he pinched the skin on the young boy's arm and twisted it as hard as he could. Billy shuddered and felt the heat of tears pooling in the corners of his eyes. "If you so much as try and chase after your mother, I'll skin you both raw in the night."

The boy said nothing, his tongue had stopped working. A trickle of urine ran down his inner thigh and puddled on the floor by his feet. He screamed silently inside as he watched the old man trot out of the room on all fours, in search of something evil.

The old man returned to the room. bipedal once more, with a meat cleaver and length of rope from the garage in one hand and a bucket full of ice in the other. "All I want are your kidneys," the old man barked through his snouted grin, from his punctured soul.

The boy, now a wreck, turned to look at the packet of sweets on the table, panicking—how could he somehow stall this old man? Maybe he could get upstairs to Grandma and tell him about how cruel Granddad was being. Or, if he could find the key, he could escape. He could run with the wolves who were stronger, faster than the foxes, back to his mother. How he wished he'd told her the truth at the start, when he knew that Granddad was sick.

"C... could I have just one sweet first? P... please, Granddad?" the boy managed to force out.

Granddad looked at the packet on the table and dumped his tools in a pile.

"I do like a butter candy," he said, his eyes cunning, darting, plotting.

He opened the packet and sat down slowly in his corner chair. Billy moved to a far corner of the room, putting as much distance between himself and the old man as he could. He didn't want to be anywhere near the hideous beast, for this man was the stuff of nightmares. This man was worse than the fox with its stinking guts draped in the dust. He was the stranger they warned him to stay away from at school. He was the evil that the night brings.

Billy looked at the clock on the mantelpiece—the only clock in the world with the apparent power to slow down time—his mother wouldn't be back for another eleven hours.

Granddad popped out his carnivorous fangs and dropped them into a crystal glass on the table by his chair.

"Want one then, Billy?" Granddad laughed, proffering the dish to the boy. "Did you piss your pants?"

Billy's mouth was far from watering, it felt drier than the desert—and his stomach was tied in a tight, empty knot.

"Do you want a sweet, boy?" Granddad hollered a second time as Billy cowered, unused to the generosity, knowing it most likely was a trap.

"Come here, boy. Take a sweet," he howled. Billy edged forward; perhaps the old man was offering him a final supper? Was there a residue of kindness in this old man's desperate rock of a

30

heart? He tried to ignore the cleaver, the rope and the ice bucket on the other side of the room.

He reached out a shaking young arm —through fear of disobedience over any type of hunger—and tried to take a sweet, but Granddad's clawed paw yanked the bag back and away. Billy recoiled and felt fresh tears welling up, disappointed that he'd fallen for one of Granddad's mean tricks again. "Over my dead body, you little shit!" said Granddad, laughing a gummy laugh.

Granddad tossed a candy up into the air and tilted his wrinkled head back. He caught the sweet in his mouth, but it travelled a little too far. The sweet lodged tight—a plug in the hole, a ship in a bottle—in the back of the old man's wasted throat. It sat blocking his airways. The old man knew straight away what'd happened and jumped up from his chair like a youth. He put his hands on his scraggy neck and, wide-eyed, approached the little boy who stood wet in the front room. The boy looked up at his grandfather, who was now very red in the face, fast becoming a bloody gargoyle of a man.

Then Billy looked at the clock on the mantelpiece and wished it would tick a little slower.

The old man started to gag and foam collected at the sides of his mouth. Sweets scattered all over the floor. His eyes bulged, bloodshot, as he continued to struggle for air. He reached around and pointed at his own spine, indicating where the

31

boy should slap him hard between the shoulder blades.

The boy sat tight.

The man's body started to spasm as the old rotter fell on all fours and then to the floor. His frail limbs were writhing around, a nest of snakes, as his hands clamped around his own neck, pummelling and probing and trying to push out the sweet. All to no avail. A grey-pink tongue thrust forwards and backwards from his dribbling face hole, now no longer a fox, but a lizard tasting the air. His eyes rolled back and shook and looked fit to burst from their sockets as his pensioner's spine arched and twisted. The old git was helpless and the boy watched the show from the sofa.

"All I wanted you for was your toffees," the boy said, in words as sharp and clear as the crystal cut glass in which the old man's teeth were still swimming. The lad bent forward and collected a toffee from the floor which he unwrapped and popped into his mouth; the sweet taste flooding his chops. His tongue shouted out with joy, his kidneys screamed with freedom, but his lips spoke nothing further of it all that day and neither did the old man's. Billy crunched down hard on the candy with his tough young teeth, turned his head away from the silenced mess on the floor and sat and watched the turning hands of the mantelpiece clock.

Billy started to gather the loose sweets, putting each back into the bag and another into his mouth. In time with the hand on the mantelpiece clock, he heard his Grandmother's footsteps. Grandma was coming down the stairs. He panicked. She'd asked why he hadn't called for her, why he hadn't tried to save Granddad. All the blood in his body rushed straight toward the floor as he started to feel dizzy with panic and guilt. Would he end up in prison for what had done, or what he had chosen to ignore? He snatched up the last few candy wrappers from the table and floor and shoved them back into the bag, then shoved the bag in the old dusty vase on the mantelpiece aside the clock whose ticks and tocks were coming harder, faster, louder. His Grandma entered the room and caught the boy toffee-handed.

"What on earth are you doing, Billy? Why are your trousers soaking wet? What was all that noise? I heard even with my useless old ears. It was louder than the foxes fighting at night in the garden."

His heart a thrumming prisoner in his throat; Billy looked around for the bucket, the knife, the rope, his frantic eyes searched for the old man's body, fastened from receiving oxygen at the top, which he was sure had been on the floor. Surely Grandma would understand if he told her the truth, if he explained everything that had happened, right from the start?

"Why are you putting candy in Granddad's urn, stuffing trash amongst his ashes?" Grandma asked; tutting and shaking her head side to side. The wrinkles in her brow rumpled, furrowed further, line on line on line.

"I—" Billy's mouth could find no words to explain how Granddad hadn't stayed at the church where his mother had said he was resting and his eyes could find no proof of the moments that had just passed at all, bar an old, heavy vase, which sat now clogged, spewing toffees and wrappers from its neck.

"Never mind, love. I'm glad he's gone," said Grandma, balancing Granddad's lid—which had slipped down behind— skew-whiff, back atop the candy stash. "Probably deserves it, anyway. You're lucky you never had the displeasure of meeting the old turd."

Smeller Feller
Sandra Stephens

Chapter I

The man lived alone. He had not always lived alone, but now he always would. He didn't know how long he would live but he knew that.

His apartment was small. A bed, a table, a chair. Some toiletries. Only overhead lights, which saturated the corners, the way he liked it. Lamps cast too many shadows.

From his place at the table where he ate, he could see the other two rooms. The living room doubled as a bedroom when the couch was folded out; he always folded the lumpy bed back into the couch in the morning, not wanting to have to worry about checking under the bed during the day.

The bathroom was a simple tub with an attached shower head, a porcelain toilet stool with no lid and a cracked porcelain sink. The new shower curtain was clear; before, it had been white. He tried to remember to bunch it up at the back of the tub, so nothing could lurk within. But he sometimes forgot and found himself increasingly obsessed with checking it. He began to dream of it, always finding it pulled around the tub, his hand reaching toward the curtain to yank it back, hearing the breathing behind it, the peculiar long inhales. An exhalation of graves.

Were the dreams a warning? His subconscious picking up cues, perhaps detecting disturbances in the air in the apartment building lobby, or a dissipated smell in the long narrow hallway outside his front door.? A sound of footsteps pacing the late night street as he slept his fitful sleep?

After installing the clear curtain the dreams receded. He might not have to move again. It would be the eighth time in two years. He was tired.

He looked older than he was and was younger than he felt. His father, a judge, also had prematurely gray hair. But his own hair was not graying, he knew. It was whitening. Had been, ever since the weekend two years ago when he first met the man with a name like a creature in a storybook. A name he'd laughed at, the first time he heard it: the Smeller Feller.

Two years and four thousand miles later, he wasn't laughing now.

Chapter II

At first he had not understood how everything had changed, wouldn't have believed it if forewarned and in fact didn't believe it, that a life could transform profoundly in the space of one breath - one long stinking inhale - to the next. He had not always been gifted with the imagination he currently possessed.

He rarely spoke to anyone anymore. He never lived anywhere long enough to make friends, not that he could have maintained them. Then there was the matter of his breath.

There was no objective reason for his breath to be bad. He stuck to bland foods, brushed and flossed and used mouthwash but after a few hours the scent of mint would acquire a sour undertone.

He'd begun to notice people were moving away slightly from him when in close proximity, but whether this was due to his appearance or his smell he couldn't be sure. All his clothes were purchased at second hand and thrift stores. Unwilling to visit a barber, he had let his hair and beard grow; he dreaded the thought of another human being getting close to his face, smelling him. Inhaling hundreds, maybe even thousands of the 40,000 dead skin cells humans supposedly lost every day. If that was true, if someone took a deep enough sniff, they in a way became a part of you. If

37

enough people breathed in enough of his dead skin cells, maybe the Smeller Feller (he didn't like even thinking the name) would catch wind of him.

In Paris, he found the answer. Beneath Paris was another Paris; the catacombs and sewers of Paris were boulevards of the dead and the dirty. He stood in a small tour group listening to the tour guide, not put off in the least by the low feral stink of the sewers. For the first time in months, he could stand near people and they wouldn't think twice about a bad smell emanating nearby; they expected it.

"The dislike of odours from bodily fluids across cultural boundaries may be an evolutionary response," said the guide. "A way to avoid disease. We don't like the smell of shit because our nose tells us it will make us sick." She paused.

"You could say, modernity rose on the strength of the nose."

He burst into startled laughter; even he heard the note of hysteria in it that caused some of the other tourists to step away from him.

The guide, a pretty young woman, looked his way and smiled at the success of her little joke. To his surprise she invited him for coffee at the end of the tour. He accepted, glad for the company, not having spoken in nearly a week.

The cafe had two glass walls, giving him plenty of sightline without being obvious about keeping a lookout. She smoked a constant chain of cigarettes, masking the faint mouldy mineral smell of him. Or so he thought, until she excused herself to go to the restroom. Just before she rose, for just a second, her nose wrinkled and she looked down at herself.

He knew what she was thinking: that she smelled like the sewers. She didn't, though. She smelled, he thought, like a mixture of cake batter and sadness. He had been trying all afternoon to not too obviously sniff her.

The smell was coming from him. It always got stronger when he'd been located. The fear he'd been located probably made it even stronger.

"I must go now," she declared after an hour and a half. She offered her hand in the American style rather than the typical French cheek kiss but whether because of her supposed odour - or his - or lack of interest in him, he didn't know. It didn't matter. A relationship was out of the question, though a place to escape to if the Smeller Feller found him was a good idea. Or so he thought, until the dream.

They were at his place, watching a movie on the foldout bed. The covers were a bird's nest. The TV was new, the box still on the floor. She wore one of his t-shirts, a pair of his boxers. Her hair a sexy post-coital mess. He liked his dream.

The French girl went to the bathroom and there was the cosy sound of water filling the tub. After a while, his dream self-paused the movie - American Beauty, one of his favourites in his dreams as well as real life, apparently - and went to the kitchen. He poured a glass of red wine for her, a Bière de Garde for himself, pushing open the bathroom door with his backside to find the curtain - the old opaque white one, not the clear replacement he'd installed - partially drawn around the tub.

Somewhere deep in his dreamer's subconscious, faint alarm bells went off.

"Madame, your wine." From behind the curtain came indescribable noises. His mind screamed He found you, run! even as he watched his hand pull the shower curtain back to reveal the Smeller Feller crouched over the French girl's flayed open midsection like a floating charcuterie board, a huge grin splitting his face, his teeth like bones poking up from the graves of the rising dead.

The sensation of the bottle slipping from his numb fingers felt as real as the foam spilling its fresh stinging yellow beer scent down his leg so that when he woke with the smell strong in his nose he screamed, unable to locate himself in reality, one arm up to shield himself from the terrible sight, the other finally locating his bedside lamp switch and creating a pool of light in the dark and revealing the source of the smell: he'd wet the bed. His heart galloping, he checked every nook and cranny of the apartment. He listened at his door and heard no scrape of a shoe, no sound of breathing.

He texted the girl Are you alright? Then changed alright to awake.

He fell asleep watching his phone for an answering text, feeling a low grade comfort in the connection even if it was unfulfilled on her end. The fact that she waited until morning to text him back told him just how much he'd changed, how ragged he'd become.

He asked to meet her again at the same cafe but when they arrived, found it closed. The sky spat cold drops.

"We can always meet back tomorrow when it's open again," he said, wanting only to get inside, out of the open street with its multiple alleys and driveways.

It was the right thing to say, the thing that seemed to put her feelings first, even if it didn't.

"I live nearby," she said in an "I'll take the plunge" tone of voice that normally would have him feeling victorious, but the dream was too recent and he was too nervous about standing out in the open.

Her flat was one large room with a fire escape, her double bed tucked in the far corner from the door under the shadowy eaves of a slanted ceiling. An antique crystal chandelier hung in the centre of the room like an Old World disco ball. On one wall, a life size poster of a model in a gown made entirely of flowers, holding an intricate bottle of perfume.

Her father, she told him, was a chemist for a major perfume house, the nose behind a dozen high end fragrances.

"How does the daughter of a perfume creator end up working in a place that smells like shit?"

41

She laughed. "You Americans, always talking about work. Did you know that smells are stored as memories? It's true. Until I left university, I studied chemistry, to follow in my father's footsteps, naturellement."

"Where did you study?"

Her eyes slid away from his. "Yale. But I dropped out with just two years."

"Why? America not your cup of tea?"

"Men are not my cup of tea."

He opened his mouth to comment but she ignored him, continuing.

"Four particular men. From one particular night."

His mouth snapped close.

"I think there were four," she added, like a bayonet. "They drugged me, of course, so I can't be sure."

As she spoke she prepared coffee in a French press and toasted some bread in a countertop toaster oven. The fierce sound of the bean grinder filled the air.

"I was wearing one of my father's perfumes that night. Now, when I smell fragrance…" She gave an eloquent shrug, pulled the toasted bread out, put it on a plate with butter and jam.

"I'm sorry," he whispered.

"C'est la vie. Many women have the same story, only the details are different. The smell of perfume makes me feel dead. Now, I fill my life with different scents that tell me I am alive. Like shit and bread."

She took a deep inhale and the sound of air whistling in her nostrils made him flinch, prickling his skin into goose bumps. He felt his eyes flood with tears, though for her or himself he wasn't sure.

She touched his arm. "And now we have come to it, the time for you to tell me what is the reason an American is in Paris looking like a dead man who walks."

She lit a new cigarette and cocked her head sympathetically. With a tremendous effort, he was able to keep further tears at bay.

"You wouldn't believe me if I told you."

"How do you Americans say? Try me."

And so with the cold fingers of the nightmare still on the back of his neck, he told her, all of it, everything from the moment two years ago when it all began at a wedding in an Appalachian holler.

***

Before then, things had been going great. An apartment with a view. Custom suits and imported shoes. The car in his garage was a Porsche 911, the girl in his bed a model, the balance in his bank account climbing to new heights every month, thanks to all the new clients the model had introduced him to.

They met at a coke-fueled party in the Hamptons. You sound like home, she said of his

43

Ohio accent. She was from Altoona, deep in hillbilly country. She was the guest of honour, the It girl of the year, her face on the covers of magazines, the sides of buses, a global star for the fortuitous arrangement of a few ounces of honey dipped skin, blonde hair, cartilage, and bone.

She wore her hair cut brutally short and said ewe instead of you, the way his sister had. The camera loved her.

The man was from a big family and couldn't understand why anyone would willingly give up their privacy to the degree that the model did.

No thanks, he told the model when she asked if he too wanted a big family someday. I'm not really the family guy type, he said with a crooked smile. He'd learned this admission did not always turn women off - at least, not the kind of women he wanted to be with.

Same, said the model. Her mama would kill her, she said, if she caught pregnant now that she was making so much money modelling. He thought she might be the perfect woman.

When her cousin got married, she invited him to go back to the homestead as her date for the wedding, a weekend long party with family coming in from all over.

"It's goin' to be a real hootenanny," she drawled.

They drove the winding roads into Appalachian hill country in the model's Ferrari, a gift from one of her many admirers, probably one of the assholes at the Hamptons party. The man enjoyed the sound of the billions of tiny stones chattering against the undercarriage, perhaps chipping the paint. He wondered why anyone would give a woman such a gift just for ass. Paying for ass - even indirectly - was for assholes, was his view.

Bugs plastered themselves against the dust-coated windshield. He glimpsed the occasional house or trailer or weed-bound truck on flattening tires. They growled past rutted side roads and byways, where the tracks of previous travellers were more a suggestion of a suggestion of a path than a path. Down one of these, a dark shape caught his eye, a man so tall he gave a confused impression of a tree escaping the forest. In his surprise, the car slowed infinitesimally; at the same moment, the walker's head lifted, revealing the great bony moon of his face.

In bare seconds the car was through the intersection, the side road in the rear view.

"Creeping Jesus," he said, in his startlement resurrecting a favourite curse of his father's. "What the hell was that?"

Cognitive dissonance washed over him; he wished, simultaneously, to back the car up and gaze at the figure slicing darkly through the humid air and also accelerate quickly away, to be around the next bend before the walker reached the T junction. He kept his eye on the rear view mirror, half expecting to see the dark man emerge onto the road and turn left to follow them. But the road remained empty except for the cloud of dust they'd just kicked up.

"Who was what?" The model, slouched in her seat, didn't look up from her phone.

"He looked like Ichabod Crane come to life," he said. Or the last horseman of the apocalypse after he killed and ate his horse, he thought to himself.

The model looked at him blankly. "You know," she told him, "people in these parts really believe in Jesus. Better not take his name in vain."

"If that was Jesus we're all in big trouble," he laughed.

After five hours of driving he eased the car into Endless, less a town than a wide place in the road with a one-room church complete with a stark wooden cross on its roof, a post office with a dusty closed sign in the window and a single gas pump. Benches were stacked on the porch of the church. Three old men sat in wooden rocking chairs in the dusty forecourt of the gas station watching barefoot kids run among stacks of tires, pursuing kittens.

In front of the church was a dirt yard and single wooden pole. On top of the pole was a black brimmed hat with a dented round crown.

"Uh oh," said the model upon spying it. "Looks like someone's gonna be in trouble!" She sang the last word, like a child: truh-bull!

Before he could ask what she meant she was out of the car and joining the kids chasing the kits and greeting everyone in the clearing by name. The pump attendant was a red-headed boy who emitted a loud keening ki-yi-yi-yi when he saw the model, who he called baby cousin.

While they talked, the man had a look around the tiny perimeter, feeling the eyes of the old gents as he peered inside the front windows of the post office and the church. The wooden benches stacked on the school-church porch looked hand hewn. There were carvings on the seats, he saw. Let the thief no longer steal. O let the evil of the wicked come to an end. Come not down the lanes or in our meadows.

The model's family homestead was a scattering of houses and sheds with a pasture, barn, a pond fed by a creek and land that was still mostly forest. The model exited the car with a flurry of elbows and long legs, squealing names and suddenly people were pouring out of the house and barn.

A girl with a strong resemblance to the model, a milkweed blonde instead of brunette, broke from the melee. "Are you Sissy's boyfriend?"

"Sure," he said.

She was several notches shorter and heavier than the model. In her too-tight midi-top and her too-short shorts she gave off an impression of bursting with juicy life.

"Baby sister, give me a huuuuug!!" the model hollered and the girl slid away, rubbing against the side of the car like a cat.

"Be seeing you," she smirked.

Maybe this weekend would be more interesting than he thought.

A steady stream of visitors arrived and the man took a few pictures to add to the cache he kept on an encrypted thumb drive. He thought of the thumb drive - which was designed to look like a sleek little bottle opener and which he carried with him always on his key ring - as an insurance policy. Pictures like these and far more intimate pictures and videos (most the model was aware of but some most definitely not) could be worth something someday - especially the one in which she passed out so solidly that as he worked over her body he began to think that he was doing her a favour, monitoring her breathing which had become shallow enough to be almost concerning. In the end she was fine, sleeping deeply for 18 hours and waking up with almost no memory, apologizing for throwing up and after all he didn't do anything to her while passed out she hadn't agreed to when sober and with total enthusiasm, of which he even had proof.

"Is it true you saw him?" the sister watched him with a laser beam intensity that made his shoulder blades twitch.

There was no reason for the word "him" to evoke the briefly glimpsed black tree-man walking down the road. No reason to picture his bony

48

cadaverous face. No reason to suddenly realize the man in black wore the same hat as the one on the pole in the clearing.

"How did you know?"

"My sister texted me asking if I knew who Ichabod Crane was."

"So you're a reader." His sister Gemma had loved The Headless Horsemen. He had read it to her every Halloween when they were kids.

"I've read every book in the summer bookmobile," she said.

"Maybe I'll send you some," he said, offhandedly.

"Yeah sure maybe you will," she said. "But you saw him, right? With your own eyes?"

"Barely - he was pretty far away. What is he, a priest or something?"

"Not hardly. The priest doesn't know if you sinned unless you confess and then he still can't do anything about it, on account of confession being a sacrament. You can murder someone and tell a priest and still get away with it. With the Smeller Feller, no one gets away with nothin."

"What the hell is a Smeller Feller?"

"It's THE Smeller Feller," she corrected him, adding. "there's just one, thank gawd. He finds wrongdoers."

"And how does he know who did wrong?"

"He can smell it, silly." She said it matter of factly, as if she believed it.

He burst out laughing. She didn't seem bothered.

"You're telling me he smells if you've been bad or good? Is he the Appalachian version of Santa, or what?" He chuckled at his own witticism. But she was serious.

"Usually someone calls for him. KatieLynn, the bride, was fit to be tied, everyone knows, havin the Smeller Feller around the day before your weddin' is the worst kind of bad luck. But old man Wallace said no waitin' on such things."

"What things?"

"Sarey Wallace got herself in the family way. Wallace wants to know who did her like that, with her just twelve."

A car honked outside, then another. There was a general sense of movement, people flowing out to the yard.

"Come on, then," the girl told him, waggling her eyebrows. "Smellin' time."

They joined a stream of people walking down the road. More people emerged from the side roads. Soon it was a sizable group.

"So you all just line up, or what?" He couldn't picture anyone actually standing still while being smelled for wrongdoing, unless it was by one of those drug sniffing dogs at the airport, backed up by an armed DEA agent.

"Well today, just the men and the boys."

"Even me? I've only been here a few hours. That's not enough time to get someone pregnant, even on my best day." But she didn't laugh with him.

"There's no getting out of it. If you don't show up with the rest of the men, he'll come find you."

"You definitely don't want the old smeller feller sniffin' around, huntin' you down," the model chimed in. "Not unless you feel like wettin' the bed."

"What about, uh…" he laid a finger on his nostril and made a quick sniff. He meant drugs of course - what about the drugs they'd been doing. He was trying to keep his voice low but the model threw back her head and laughed loudly.

"Honey lamb", she said, her voice dripping with southern syrup. "Coke ain't no sin, it's just illegal. It's sinners he's after. Wrongdoers."

He estimated about four dozen people were walking with them by then. Some kids on bikes, dirt bikes and battered old ATVs zoomed ahead and looped back, until they'd all been corralled into the gas station clearing.

Someone had set up the benches in rows of four on two sides of the clearing. A wooden table was on the third side where three men stood, all wearing black hats with round crowns, the same as the hat on the pole. One of them nodded and the model elbowed him; only then did he recognize them as the same men sitting on the porch of the gas station mart. It was unnerving, he thought, how such an innocuous item of clothing could give them such gravitas.

The girl stood with her back against the pole in a faded yellow dress and cheap rubber sandals, her pregnancy as high and round as a basketball. She wore her red hair in two tails, like his kid sister Gemma had favoured the summer she stepped, carefully and holding a fist full of dandelions, in front of a train.

The women were taking their seats on the benches. One of the three men with hats cleared his throat.

"I reckon everyone knows the drill. Remember, at least one arm's length apart between you and the next guy, that's in front of you and behind you too. Give him room to work. If you got a cap, take it off, same with what's in your pockets. No talking, speak only if spoken to, but there's some who would recommend not even then and I'm one of them. Under eight or over eighty you can sit this one out. When everyone's in line Larch will ring the summons."

The old guy spoke and the men began handing things to wives and mothers and daughters - hats, phones, keys, round containers of Skoal, pocket knives.

"Just think about something nice," the model whispered as he handed her his phone and keys.

"Fix on a good memory and don't let go of it," the sister added.

He found himself in a shuffling group of men that gradually arranged itself into three rows, with him in the back and seriously considering stepping

52

backward slowly until he reached the woods, until he looked over and caught the warning eye of the model's sister who gave her head a little shake. Idly he wished he'd had the presence of mind to do a couple of lines before the show started. As if on cue, one of the men rang the school bell.

The men were quiet. There was the song of insects and the small buzzing of an occasional fly. Here and there, weight shifted from one foot to the other, gravel creaking under shoes. The women waited, adjusting little ones on their laps and keeping a hand or eye on toddlers, but they did so quietly, with warning fingers to lips and the kids sat mostly still and looked into their laps at toys or things from their pockets and made no sound.

It was a late spring day, but if there was a breeze he didn't remember it later. He heard the caw cawing of a faraway bird. This was followed by more silence and then another caw from another, less far away bird and another closer still and then the sound - gradually building so that at first he thought it was his imagination - of dozens of little things skittering through the underbrush in the woods adjacent to the road. The minute sounds of sticks breaking and leaves crunching and branches snapping as rabbits and squirrels and quail and snakes and frogs and even insects made an almost musical exodus that lasted for a few minutes before trickling off and becoming quiet again, the quiet shaping itself around the sound of footsteps that rang against the composition surface of the road like handclaps of the dead, getting closer with each long step, that rang out clearly even with the ravens calling overhead.

He glanced around; no one met his eye but the model's sister, who mouthed NO, SHHH to him just as the Smeller Feller strode into the clearing and the impulse to laugh dried in his mouth like a dead thing.

Whatever it said about him as a man, he was able to admit to himself the only thing keeping him in the clearing when the Smeller Feller arrived was the utter immobility of the other men. Had even one began to run, he would have quickly followed suit. But everyone stayed put, in fact so still that to move even a little would be to call attention to himself, which he felt that he did not want to do despite the very strong lobbying by his newfound friends to leave now, while all eyes were riveted on the man who could smell sin.

He estimated the Smeller Feller was close to seven and a half feet tall, with the kind of angular face and prognathic brow he associated with college basketball players not finished with their growth spurts. His black coat fell from the wide rack of shoulders that were thin without being the least bit frail. His skin was waxy whitish yellow with a bluish undertone visible at the edges, stretched tight over the bones of his long face. His nose was enormous, even given the size of the face it was part of. It was blade shaped, as tall as it was long, aquiline at the top, with a bony nodule in the middle of the bridge and nostrils flaring into great dark crevasses, dense with a forest of black cilia that undulated in the current of his breath.

The Smeller Feller stood for a moment staring - first at the seated women, then at the standing men. There was no shuffling of feet, no scratching of noses or rubbing of chins. No tongues licked dry lips. In the shadow of the stiff brim of his hat, his dark eyes in their deep eye sockets were like individual animals peering out, seeming to take them all in while singling each one of them out.

Around the man an odour was rising, as the adrenal glands of the men released epinephrine and cortisol into bloodstreams. Hearts pumped harder, blood pressure increased, opening wide the airways in the men's lungs and narrowing blood vessels in their skin and intestines to increase blood flow to their major muscle groups.

The Smeller Feller moved first to the girl Sarey who stood staring at the ground before her swollen feet, both arms supporting the bulk of her pregnancy. He seemed to cover the ground to her in just a couple of steps, as if his legs were stretching sneaky extra inches at the end of every stride he took.

He stood close to her, looming, bending low from his waist to hover over the top of her head the way a chef might hover over a kettle of soup, eyes closed, taking in her scent. Bringing that awful proboscis low to her head, he sniffed her crown, along her hairline and down the ruler-straight middle of her part, leaving a light snail trail of mucus that gleamed in the sun. He spent long minutes in front of her face, breathing in her breaths with a slurpy kind of greed. He spent even longer minutes at her pregnant belly and below and the man turned his eyes away, appalled with a prudery he hadn't known he possessed.

The Smeller Feller continued until the end of his ministrations; the girl sagged a little more with each sniff. Though her face maintained a stoic expression, tears leaked from her eyes, as if she were crying despite herself. When her legs crumpled, two of the black hat men were at her side to catch her by her elbows. The Smeller Feller leaned forward and put his mouth close to the girl's ear and she whined a little and pulled away, the way someone would when hearing electronic feedback, or smelling a sudden bad smell. But she was nodding, too. Crying and squinching up her face in pain and nodding in a way that was resigned or relieved.

The men half-carried her to a ladder-back chair that had been brought from the church, where she sat with hands covering her face, the women clustered around her and patting her back.

The black hatted man called Larch cleared his throat and looked up at the sky.

"What needs to be known will be known," he said. The women repeated it, their voices as one.

"What needs to be done will be done," Larch said and the women repeated that too.

Staring up at the clouds, Larch next addressed Sarey's abuser.

"You are known to yourself and two others. Step forward now to atone for your sins and be known to us all."

"For as you do ill to one of us, so do you do ill to us all," said the women. Some were crying.

With a speed the man found deeply unsettling, the Smeller Feller's dark legs scissored to the front of the first row of men, his head hawked forward in that strangely hungry way. Closer, he looked even taller, the sockets of his eyes a touch too wide for his eyes, the sclera grey and ancient looking, like cracked boulders.

Jesus Christ how old is he? the man wondered. As if sensing the thought (or smelling it) the Smeller Feller's eyes fell on him like a physical weight. He stood stock still in the third row with two men between them, breathing as shallowly as possible. He was aware of his heartbeat - the thud in his ears, speeding up. When the Smeller Feller's eyes slid away it was a sensation he could feel, like a buzzard taking flight after resting on his shoulder.

A few minutes ago you were laughing and comparing him to Santa, he reminded himself, but there was no hilarity in the thought. Fear - real fear! he thought, amazed - had opened up inside him like a sinkhole. There was a feeling of having slipped sideways into one of the Brothers Grimm stories that in better days his kid sister Gemma insisted he read to her again and again - stories that always took place in the woods, he remembered. Though in those stories, like real life, it wasn't the woods that hurt you but the people hiding out in them.

The Smeller Feller took a long inhale, his nose a sail of bone and waxy skin that surfed the air, as if rummaging through many scents. The twin tunnels of his gross nostrils distended, bellowsing almost daintily, the visible black hairs bending to and fro like reeds before a river of stinky wind. Watching them, the man felt his own hair raise a little in response, but surely that was his imagination, no man could inhale so deeply he made another's hair stand on end from twelve feet away?

But the feeling persisted, felt not only in the androgenic hair covering his head and chest and arms prickling upright but the nearly invisible vellus hair on his ears and the nape of his neck and even the strands sprouting from the areola around his nipples were indisputably moving, standing on end, pulling away from his body towards the Smeller Feller. When he felt his nose hairs stirring he had to restrain a powerful urge to rub his knuckles against the tickle.

Now the Smeller Feller walked before the first row of men, inhaling them each in turn, sometimes in long snoring nasal inhales that whistled, other times with the thin liverish lips parted, sucking air over teeth that were as oversized and strong-looking as the rest of him. In a parody of intimacy he leaned in close to mouths and noses and ears, sniffing breath and mucus and ear wax with obscene avidity.

With each inhalation, the man felt a tiny tickle, a pulling sensation deep in the center of his skull, like a rotten virtual tooth loose and wiggling in its socket.

The Smeller Feller smelled his way down the line. For such a tall man he was agile, his questing head almost eel-like as he followed his nose around the personal scentscape of each man. His tongue came out at the apex of each inhale, as if the air and its freight of sin were a physical thing, pushing the tip out past the barrier of his tombstone teeth so that it protruded and hid, protruded and hid, questing, slug-like. The man thought he'd never seen a more repulsive face, so alive and dead at the same time. It was as if the longer he looked, the more he could see - the skin with its forehead furrowed by warts, the ears with the sprouting hairs, tiny dead insects trapped in a dandruff of earwax. His gorge rose and he turned his eyes away.

As the Smeller Feller's inhalations continued, a distinct odour arose, like the rush of bad air at a long-sealed crypt. Inhaling it, the man had a sudden memory of a teacher in the sixth grade with persistent bad breath, Mrs. Sautman, the kids called her Sourbreath Sautman and Mrs. Shitbreath behind her back. Or rather he did and the other kids followed, or might get a charley horse or wedgie during recess. Once, he returned to the classroom to get his lunch and heard crying in the coat closet, opening the door to find Mrs. Sautman sobbing while opening a green roll of Winto'green lifesavers. Her tear-filled eyes never left his as she peeled the paper and foil back and thumbed the top candy into her mouth and the sharp wintergreen smell when she crunched did not drown out the smell of her breath concentrated in the closet, or the hatred in her eyes.

Somewhere down the line a sound of sobbing, muffled like Mrs. Sautman, pressed behind lips instead of coats. Three more men until his turn.

With each of the Smeller Feller's inbreaths - whether the long lung-busting inhales or the grotesque short snuffling sounds like a pig hunting truffles - the man felt a slight internal physical-mental tugging sensation. As if his thoughts were nails, spilled from one of his dad's old paint cans and the Smeller Feller's inhales were like the giant U-shaped red and silver magnet his dad kept in his toolbox. If you held the magnet at the right distance, the pile of jumbled nails would tremble, ready to be collected by the magnet.

I have nothing to worry about, he told himself, looking over at the girl Sarey, sitting in the shade now, looked after by some of the women, one of them the model's sister.

Nothing at all.

It was true in the legal sense, of course. But the Smeller Feller - who had now arrived in front of the guy to the man's right - wasn't a lawyer.

Jesus you're not actually worried about this guy smelling you, are you?

He was.

The stink was stronger now, whether coming from the Smeller Feller drawing close or because so many men were releasing the musk of fear (or sin) at the same time - or some combination of the two - the man wasn't sure. He tried breathing in through his mouth and out through his nose, facing forward with an expression he hoped made him look sympathetic yet slightly annoyed, tolerant yet impatient. Forbearing, but not from here.

He tried to clear his mind but thoughts like little nails kept flying free from the jumble, as though drawn out by the irresistible force of the Smeller Feller's probing inhales. His purpose. People - women - he hadn't thought of in years. The pregnant girlfriend he broke it off with, moving to a new job and new city without telling her and changing his cell phone number for good measure. The countless pre-dawn bedrooms he had quietly dressed in, slipping out the door with shoes in hand. The affair with his partner's wife. The passed out sorority girl he photographed, then shared the photos around. The boss he seduced then anonymously reported, getting her fired and himself promoted. The woman now passing his child off as her husband's.

Jesus, he told himself. Of all the things to be thinking about! He tried to picture the model, but her face morphed into that of his college girlfriend sobbing at his door in the middle of the night, desperate at his cool detachment. Letting her stumble away without checking to see if she was okay to drive, or even how she got there. The way he treated the call girls in Vegas. Jesus.

He tried to jerk his mind back to the present, with limited success; the memories bobbed like long-submerged corpses to the surface of a lake. The smell was now strong enough he surreptitiously held his breath. As soon as he did so, the flood of memories stopped. But how long could he hold his breath?

Fix on a good memory and don't let go of it.

An image of Gemma, ponytailed, looking like Sarey Wallace without the distended belly. The summer before her final, fatal step they spent a lot of time in the barn, always a few degrees cooler. Climbing into the haymow gave a view of nearly the whole county, mostly farmer's fields, a vision he secretly thought looked like a giant's game board.

Do you believe in heaven? she had asked and he, though just fifteen, did not have the heart to answer truthfully, so said instead, Maybe this is it, right here, heaven on earth and she agreed. Heaven would most definitely smell like horses was her view and though he teased her that an eternity of shovelling manure sounded more like hell, she would not be moved, saying only that everyone probably got the heaven they hoped for or what would be the point of heaven. She had glanced over at him to get his confirmation - he could never get over that, how she still trusted him, though he never lifted a finger to save her from what they both knew was happening at night, when the house was quiet but not silent - and that was the image the man now fixed on, grabbing it like a drowning man, the way she had looked then, smiling, her blue eyes wistful, her hair the brightest thing under the tall mid-western sky.

There was a commotion among the men. Someone stumbled forward, shrugging off the hands that tried to stay him. He was halfway across the clearing before the man recognized the ginger headed boy from the gas station. The boy ran, or was trying to - he hunched over as if in pain, a forearm held against his stomach. Even a hundred feet away he could smell the ginger's sweaty stink of desperation, a mix of singed hair, burnt tires, piss and tobacco.

That's what guilt smells like, the man thought.

"Jamie, stop," called Sarey. "Oh, someone, please stop him." The women rapidly closed around her like a flower closing up its petals and her tear streaked face was blocked from the man's view.

Larch stepped into the clearing, to the hat pole, and clapped his hands together once and everyone looked to him, waiting. The man noticed the liquid speed of the Smeller Feller's head when it turned and felt his knees go weak.

"We know what we need to and we'll give what we are bound," he said.

"Come not down the lanes or in our meadows." The voices of the women and men were sudden and loud in the stillness.

The Smeller Feller's mouth dropped open. The voice that issued forth was deep, as if made from the metals at the core of the earth, crackled with the static of galaxies, echoing with dimensions.

"For thy peace, I pawn my own soul."

Still holding his breath, the man could feel the bass note of that voice vibrating in his bones.

The Smeller Feller walked after the ginger, his legs eating up the ground in big dusty bites. In seconds, he was out of sight. For maybe a minute no one moved or spoke. A bird chirped; then another. The cicadas resumed their afternoon song. The men returned to their women and collected their belongings. Some had damp hairlines, some had great sweat marks on the backs and underarms of their shirts. There was some talking in low voices. With all of this movement arose another smell as it became clear that more than a few had pissed themselves, and worse.

They went home the way they got there, walking. No one mentioned the ginger boy or what might be happening to him. The man felt too relieved to have escaped being smelled to want to say anything at first; what he needed was a drink, a feeling that seemed to be shared once the wedding reception got underway. Whether it was due to the pressure release from the trial-by-Smeller Feller, or genuine happiness for the wedded bliss of the young couple, everyone seemed to be drunk, even the Larch fellow, now hatless and tipped back in a porch chair, his head thrown back and his mouth open to passing June bugs.

It was a convivial time, but every time the man tried to steer the conversation to what had happened in the clearing and speculate on the fate of the ginger, someone changed the subject and handed him another drink, until he eventually forgot to ask, stumbling to bed in the wee hours and sleeping the dreamless sleep of the spectacularly drunk. He woke up before dawn with the beginnings of a hangover and a raging need to urinate.

He stood before the toilet, his stream sounding loud enough to wake the whole house and sure enough, the creak of someone opening a door and steps coming down the hall could be heard, stopping outside the door.

"Be right out," he whispered.

The person waiting sniffed, exhaling impatiently. As his seemingly endless stream continued, there came another sniff - longer and deeper.

Much, much longer.

He felt his scalp prickle, a feeling like nails all trembling at once in the presence of a magnet.

The third inhalation awoke a faint tugging sensation in his gut. The Smeller Feller was outside the door, inhaling.

He went cold, his poor penis trying to shrink right out of his hand. His urine stream dried up.

The sound of the door knob turning left, then right, then left. As he stared at it, still gripping himself, there was a snuffling sound at the bottom of the door and he grinned at himself in the dark. The fucking dog having a late night stroll down the hallway.

He put his ear near the door, listening... and from the top of the twelve foot door frame heard a long, deep inhale.

He tried to straighten up, step back, tuck himself in and unlock and open the door all at once. The door pulled outward and he fell with it, nearly into the arms of the model's sister.

"Holy shit," she whisper-screamed in surprise. He looked up and down the hall, but there was no one, just him and the girl.

"Very fucking funny," he snarled, not bothering to keep his voice down.

She flinched, protesting as he shouldered past her, returning to bed where he lay awake, fuming.

In the morning he took the model's car and returned early to the city, letting her figure out how she was going to get back to Manhattan - the way he saw it, a perfect payback for their little practical joke, the bitches.

That night, in his own bedroom with its view of Central Park, he reviewed the events that had transpired in Endless and felt pissed at himself for letting a bunch of hillbillies from the holler get the best of him, the model included. Her with her praline drawl. He wondered if grifters from the South had an easier time because of the charm of their accents. He'd fallen hook, line and sinker. An Ivy League city slicker with a penthouse in Manhattan - he guessed he represented the perfect stooge for the whole 'smelling' setup.

It was psychosomatic, what he'd felt out there. The power of suggestion - the kid sister setting him up perfectly. The Smeller Feller guy was no different than the charlatans that traveled around selling Professor Munslow's High Energy Elixir, or healing the afflicted. A guy like that, so tall and unique looking, was a natural showman. And you could achieve amazing effects with makeup and prosthetics these days. He'd even thought, himself, what a difference a mere hat could make.

Then there was the model's sister, planting the seed. What had she said? "There's no getting out of it. If you don't show up with the rest of the men, he'll come find you." That one had trouble written all over her. Probably the problem with Sarey, while he was on the subject.

As for the pulling sensation, his hairs rising on end with each of the Smeller Feller's inhales, it could have been done with a high frequency maybe, working in cahoots with the hatted guys. Or even the women.

It was an interesting idea, even a plausible idea. Even so, he could feel some little part of his subconscious resisting it, for the simple reason it didn't feel true.

The awful Smeller Feller, not plausible, nonetheless felt true.

A sliding thump in the hallway made him go still, holding his breath for long minutes. There was a distant sound of the security guard's walkie-talkie static, the sound of the stairwell door thunking closed. He relaxed.

"Boy, they got you GOOD," he jeered at himself, hoping it would make him feel sheepish and relieved (it didn't). They had, in fact, gotten him good. He lived in a building with a door man on the eleventh floor, with a security guard and cameras everywhere. There was no way anyone was getting up here to continue their little practical joke. Still, he slept with the light on. Only when the morning light and the reassuring sounds of Manhattan traffic far below flooded the room could he fully relax and fall asleep.

He jerked awake in the dimness of late afternoon, his body aware before his mind of a sound. Some sound. His eyes moved immediately to the blackout curtains that hung on the sides of the big plate glass window with its view south. Was there enough fabric to hide a man? He thought not, but could not take his eyes from the dark draperies. Were they undulating slightly, stirred by breathing?

When his phone rang, he screamed in the silence and when the curtains did not blow back to reveal the cadaverous face of the Smeller Feller bearing down on him, he might have sobbed then, but the call was from a woman he knew. No one special, just one of the dozens of women he'd had casual hook-ups with (though he always made sure to tell them they were his favourite, to maintain future access). This one was a PR flak for some minor sports star he couldn't quite remember - not as pretty as the model, but decent in the sack and, more importantly, with a big airy apartment in Brooklyn.

If anyone or anything had followed him back to the city, they would be out of luck continuing their little prank. And with no one knowing where he was, he could get a decent night's sleep. He needed it.

"You're not going to believe this," he answered her by way of greeting. "But I was just thinking about you."

He was right - the first night at the PR flak's place was the first good night's sleep he'd had in days, maybe even weeks. If she was disappointed he conked out after only one go round of lovemaking, she didn't show it. He woke up only once in the middle of the night, sure he was hearing the susurration of a stealthy inhale and exhale... and then the bed bounced lightly as the PR flak climbed back in. The susurrations resolved themselves into the sound her toilet made as it wound down its flush and he fell back asleep.

In the morning he felt better; after brunch, he felt better still. To the PR flak he was charming and attentive and beginning to convince himself he'd blown the whole thing out of proportion. It was even a little funny, a bunch of rubes getting off a good one on the city slicker. As they walked into the lobby of the PR flak's building, he thought he might tell her the whole story, when the sight of the round crowned black hat at the door man's desk stopped time.

He stared at it. The PR flak kept up her stream of chatter. The elevator continued to descend. His intestines continued to digest the eggs Benedict with salmon. But the hat just sat there, telling its implacable truth.

No one knew he was here. And yet, the Smeller Feller had been here - had somehow smelled him out.

That night he booked a redeye flight to San Francisco. The flight was less than a quarter full and the first class flight attendant had a fetching smile, but the man wasn't fetched. He had booked a first class ticket so he could board first and watch not only who boarded the plane, but what went into the plane's baggage hold.

His phone buzzed - the model texting him repeatedly, Call me. He blocked her number. He would leave his phone on airplane mode and use only taxis, not ride services that sent your location pinging to cell towers across the country. He would stay in the penthouse suite of a downtown hotel with a 360 degree view of the city, the bay and especially peninsula to the south - the direction anyone journeying on foot to the city would have to take.

It was a Tuesday. As the plane raced through the night at five hundred sixty five miles per hour at thirty five thousand feet, the man calculated: he'd be travelling a total of two thousand four hundred nineteen miles in about five hours. To drive would take nearly forty seven hours. To walk would take over one thousand hours, crossing nine states. A month and a week of days.

He pressed his head forehead against the cool plastic window. Far below, the lights of Chicago sparkled, representing millions of people in houses and apartments and office buildings, and thousands - maybe tens of thousands - of sinners - leaving the scent trails of their wrongdoing.

"Let's see you catch me now," he whispered. But quietly, under his breath and crossed himself afterwards though he hadn't been to church since Gemma's funeral.

Chapter III

As he talked the shadows grew long in the French girl's tiny room, the last of the sunset light glinting off the chandelier, the bed lost in darkness beyond it. He found he couldn't stop himself from glancing at it.

"He found me on the fourth night. In Boston. It took eleven days. Italy was the best time."

He thought he had it figured out then - an ocean between them was what it took. He never sensed him, not once - not in the noisiness of Milan, not in the quiet of Lake Como. He liked best the teeming piazzas of Florence, where he could sit alone with a coffee or a meal and be among people, scanning the crowds from behind dark glasses. He spent a weekend in Bellagio, where he met a girl, Isabella - the first woman he'd been with since the PR flak. That first morning after the first night together, he felt a cautious kind of elation. Later, he wondered if that was what drew the Smeller Feller to him - the smell of his happiness.

Even on the second night in Bellagio, when he woke to the sound of footsteps cracking along the large paver stones below, he was not at first alarmed. By then he had almost convinced himself that before the smelling (a word that always brought with it a flash of the Smeller Feller's sepulchral face) he'd been operating in a state of alcohol saturated, drug-induced paranoia and might, just might, owe the model an apology. Maybe even a thank you. He was sober now, his only drug wine with dinner and, as a result, had been sleeping better than he had in years.

He fell back asleep and dreamed (and even as he drifted into the dream didn't a watchful part of his subconscious send up a warning flare?). He was in Grand Central Terminal, the sound of air rushing, the sliding sound of feet on flooring everywhere. He boarded the train to Endless (the watchful part of his subconscious very loud now), choosing a car that was nearly empty.

At first when someone sat next to him, he just shifted without looking up, sensing rather than seeing it was a woman. When another woman sat behind him, he similarly barely noticed, distracted by his phone. It was blowing up with notifications from women he hadn't heard from in years, texting him pictures and videos and recordings of his own voice, doing and saying the most awful things. Soon a steady flow of women were coming from other cars on the train, taking the seats all round him and the seats adjacent to those. Some stood, holding the commuter hand loops or poles.

When he finally looked up and realized who the women around him were, he frantically pulled the stop cord, but the train continued, if anything speeding up. One by one they began to talk, their voices bringing the red of shame to his face. He stood and tried to push through, appalled at how many there were, appalled to hear their recollections of his worst, most private moments.

He hung on the stop cord, pulling it with all his weight and the train finally slowed, then stopped. The doors whooshed open and more women entered, doors hissing closed behind them, then bouncing open again as more women entered, each adding her awful litany to the dozens of voices.

In panic he rose and pushed his way out of the train; to his surprise, the crowd of women did not block or follow him but parted like water, letting him pass, their accusations following him like untethered balloons. The doors sighed closed and his footsteps echoed as he walked a road like the one in Endless on the day of the smelling, only instead of arriving in a clearing, it went deeper and deeper into the Appalachian forest until it became a footpath, overgrown with a thick undercover of mountain laurel and hobblebush and leading him to a place nestled deep in the darkest part of the woods, a place where the owl hooted in the daytime.

He knew without knowing how he knew that it was his place, the Smeller Feller's. A mansion of bone with a great wooden door with iron straps bracketed between ten foot columns of polished femurs, tibia, tarsals and vertebrae bound together with thin strings of human sinew.

There was no lock; he saw, maybe because it was the kind of place even a man strong enough to push open the door would not dare enter, even by invitation.

So thinking, the door juddered open with a stink of tombs.

He woke with a gasp in the darkest ditch of the night. Next to him Isabella was a vague hump with just a thatch of tousled hair visible above the covers.

Their room was on the second floor; the curtain billowed prettily at the stone window, open to the Tuscan air. He became aware of a smell - a stench he recognized instantly, though he'd smelled it only once before.

An odor of singed hair, burnt tires, piss and tobacco.

He peered over the stone sill of the window and glimpsed the top of a round crowned black hat. He quietly picked up one of the heavy terracotta pots of geraniums that lined the balcony and slowly, slowly hoisted it over his head, even as the hat crown began to slowly, slowly tip backward to reveal the bony obelisk of the Smeller Feller's face.

"Allora, cosa stai facendo amore mio?" Isabella spoke from the bed. "You are sleepwalking, come back to bed."

In the time he took to whip his head around to look at her and back at the street it was empty, the pulling sensation in his solar plexus and his forehead receded. In the street, a blue uniformed carabiniere strolled past, the heels of his uniform-issue shoes clocking his slow, deliberate progress.

Seeing the man at the window, he touched the brim of his peaked cap, his eyes expressionless.

By the time Isabella woke in the morning, he was halfway to the Milan airport, where he had booked the next available flight to Paris.

Chapter IV

"And is he here now? In Paris? You think he has he found you, this Smelling Man?"

"The Smeller Feller," he whispered. A name he always thought of in tall capital letters that cast long shadows. "I know how crazy it sounds."

"Non, not so crazy," she said. "You can forget what your eyes have seen and what your ears have heard, but you cannot forget a smell, did you know? That is because our scent memories are stored in the brain."

She tapped her temple, sending a whirlygig of smoke toward the ceiling.

"So you believe me?"

"You ask a perfumer this, pffft. It is not a matter of belief but fact, smell is our first and most developed sense. That is why the smells we love when we are children are the smells we love all our lives. Proust was right. The nose has an excellent memory."

"But do you believe me?"

She looked at him for a long time - the hollows in his cheeks, the shadows under his eyes, the new gray hairs at his temple, the weight loss that made his clothes hang on him.

"I believe you need help," she said softly. "So, I will help you the only way I know."

She handed him a box, compact and heavy. Across the front in raised purple foil letters Violetta.

"My father's latest creation," she said. "From extract of violets. The flower that symbolizes modesty, did you know? Such a romantic, my father, he feels at Yale I was not modest enough. It is better that you have it. You must change your scent, so this smeller of wrongdoing will not recognize you, oui?"

He dreamed badly that night, of a girl he hadn't thought of in years. She was just one of many high school back seat conquests, but this time, his trusty rubber emerged in shreds. The girl - Maryanne - had cried and cried, panicked she might be pregnant. He'd reassured her, irritated with himself for not knowing she'd been a virgin and took her home, never bothering to call her again, reasoning that if she did become pregnant, he'd hear from her. His last view of her was standing on her porch under the light her father had left on, wiping her eyes and fruitlessly trying to smooth the creases out of her pretty flowered sundress. In less than a week he was back at college again and definitely not thinking about high schoolers.

In the dream, he woke to the sound of long inhalations, the familiar pulling sensation in his gut and head. He followed the sound to where the opaque shower curtain was back in place, pulled closed. Somehow he was holding the potted geranium from the balcony of the Belllagio hotel room, ready to smash into the Smeller Feller's ghastly face as he yanked the curtain back to find not the smeller of his sins but a receiver of them, Maryanne. She was wearing the same flowered sundress, but it was drenched with blood, her bare legs streaked with gore.

"I tried to take care of it myself," dream Maryanne told him. She'd been dead for a few days, her jaws creaking with rigor as she spoke. He screamed, stumbling away from her as she rose; he heard the indescribable sound of her fingers slippery with blood, trying to grasp the sides of the tub. He lay on the floor, unable to move, in a kind of dream paralysis, as Maryanne crawled toward him, bringing her mouth close as if she wanted to eat him, her breath redolent of violets.

For thy peace I pawn my own soul, she moaned and he took a deep breath and held it, dream eyes shut tight, hoping like a child she'd disappear. He woke, sobbing, alone on the floor of his bathroom, the tub empty. There was a sound of rain; outside, the whispering sound of tires on the wet pavement sounded indistinguishable from long, slow breaths.

He thought he understood now. How the Smeller Feller didn't smell sin, but guilt, that miasmatic disease you couldn't see but the stink was there, ruining everything. It wasn't something he could run or move away from, or leave behind; it was in him, in his pores and would not wash away with any amount of showering. It could be covered up for a while - perfumed - but that would not change its essential nature, his essential nature.

In the morning, he shaved and trimmed his hair, doing a decent if not perfect job. He cleaned and trimmed his fingernails and toenails and pressed his clothes. He cleaned his apartment, washing the floors and even inside the oven and cabinets he barely used. When he left, the keys were on the table with a note for the landlord, a person he'd only ever communicated with by email and closed the door.

He couldn't run from the smell of his guilt any more than poor Maryanne could run from her pregnancy - or Gemma could run from hers - but at least Paris was a good walking city, especially by the rivers. He flung the thumb drive with the valuable pictures and videos of the model (now world famous, as he'd predicted) from the Ponte de Neuf and then walked along the Seine, wondering how much of it he'd get to see before the Smeller Feller caught up to him.

As a kid he'd been afraid of the water. His father, trying to cure him of this, once threw him off a boat into the cold waters of lake Michigan. He had laughed, took his time pulling the boat back to his small self, panicked and flailing in the water. He was saved in the end, but it was Gemma's and not his father's hand held out to stop him from drowning. Though he learned to swim, he never forgot that feeling, the water closing over him as he choked, waiting to see if his dad was going to save him or not.

It was hours later and falling dark when he heard the steps behind him, first synching with his own, gradually speeding up, catching up to him. Despite himself, he began to run but in his fear and exhaustion stumbled; long fingers grasped his shoulders, pulling and he flung himself forward to evade the grasp of the Smeller Feller.

His head struck a stone bench as he tumbled into the river, the sound of distant shouts muffled by the water closing over his head. A policeman's whistle sounded.

His eyes were open, looking up as he fell back into the depths, the Smeller Feller's shadow looming over him, corpse hands reaching for him, the mouth yawning open and the bass of its oxygen-less voice rattling the man's bones even as he sank. With the last of his strength he kicked away from his tormentor, the water rippling and the hatted shadow shape resolving itself in the last of the sunset light and it was not the Smeller Feller reaching and calling but a frantic carabiniere, her hat tumbling from her head as she reached for him and pulled him up and out of the river's grasp and with the water cleared from his eyes and ears he saw it was not a carabiniere at all compressing his chest, but his sister Gemma. He heard the nearby nickering of horses, smelled their warm comforting bodies, the sweet smell of hay and the mineral smell of manure. Faintly he could smell the strawberry scented shampoo his sister favored that final summer as she helped him to his feet, her copper coloured braids the brightest thing under the blue, cloud-hurled sky.

To Dust
Karl Melton

Part of Colin was aware of the portable AM/FM radio in the far corner of the busy staff lounge, but its broadcast was little more than background noise.

(The National Weather Service has issued a Dust Storm Warning for the Deming area tonight. Residents are advised to stay off the road. Extremely limited visibility is expected by…)

"I told him I left Visiting Angels for a reason. No amount of money can get me to do home visits again with horny old men. I didn't call him that, of course. Although part of me will miss his pathetic flirting attempts once he's discharged. Anyway, what are you doing tonight?" The voice belonged to Dinah, Colin's redheaded nursing colleague.

"It's Grace's Dad's birthday," Colin replied. "The big 80."

"Fun. A little senior sitting to wrap up your day of senior sitting."

"You know it."

"You better get a move on. Can't miss that," she said, her knowing eyes glistening under the bright fluorescents.

"Yeah." He hesitated, thinking of a reason good enough to stick around, even if just for a few minutes. He thought of Grace, who was likely waiting for him on the coach this very moment, doing her nervous tick that always appears whenever she has nothing to do but wait. The intermittent, three-finger tapping along the side of her right thigh, as if she were practicing her trumpet notes sans the trumpet. "Well, off to Deming, I guess," he finally said, giving a dramatic wave to Dinah. Her face gave a sympathetic smile, as if to say, what can I say other than sorry?

Colin was the one who felt sorry.

***

The smell of citrus bombarded his senses as he opened the rusted off-white metal screen door, which led into his shoddy manufactured home. He walked in to confirm his wife was not fidgeting on the coach, but in the kitchen, standing over a pitcher of purple liquid and two or three dozen squeezed limes.

"Oh hi, babe, I just finished. This batch might rival Dad's." She paused to rub her wrists. "Back when he still made them."

"Oh?" He gave her a squeeze, mindful of her baby bump. Her words, of course, since at seven months he could no longer honestly call it a bump. "That's great."

"Try some." She poured half a glass and pushed it in his face.

He did and swished the tarty concoction in the back of his mouth, mindful not to give his inevitable judgement too soon. A Texas native and self-proclaimed IPA enthusiast, he originally wasn't too crazy for the stuff Grace called a "prickly-pear margarita. Family recipe, not that mix you can buy at Allsup's," at every social gathering she had brought some to share. She first made it for him on their fourth date, back in their Baylor days when he was in nursing school and she was studying English. At some point it must have grown on him. The night of his impromptu proposal, he'd already had three of the suckers and was halfway through his fourth before the words left his mouth.

"I love you. You know that?"

"I love you too."

"I'm going to marry you."

"Then do it," she had said, a little tipsy as well.

"I will. I am. No joke. I'll buy a ring tomorrow."

"The wedding has to be in Deming. You promise?"

"You know it," he had said before carrying her to bed with drunken strength.

He'd woken up with a nasty hangover and little memory of the night before. I really need to stop drinking that sugary crap like a 6-pack of Goose. It goes straight to my head. Grace had remembered, though. Oh, she remembered and didn't think it was a joke. That night she had called her parents and he had spent half of his tuition refund at the local Jared. Little did he know tying the knot meant a permanent relocation to New Mexico.

"Tastes great, babe," he said after a while. "Just like your dad used to make them."

She let out an exaggerated sigh. "Good. I'm trusting you since I can't exactly test it myself for another two months."

Didn't stop you from trying plenty six months ago. Or two weeks ago, he thought, but he wasn't about to revive that lively discussion with her now.

Instead, he smiled and asked, "Ready to hit the road?"

Colin's '97 Camry made good time and in twenty minutes they had covered almost half the 50-mile drive down US-180.

He stole a glance at his wife. He could see the muscles in her hand tighten as she gripped the rubber case of her phone. He knew what she was thinking—why she powered on the screen every other minute. Her mother had called before on similar drives, interrupting with news that usually meant turning the car toward home. But that was then. If her phone did go off today, he had no doubt she would hang up and insist he keep driving, no matter how bad her dad was doing. For all he knew, she might even kick him out and take the wheel herself if it meant being there for her dad's birthday.

She powered on the phone again, scanning up and down, then a quick press of the power button. Rinse and repeat.

He considered mentioning that this stretch of New Mexican high desert is essentially a dead zone when it comes to phone coverage but quickly bit his tongue. He wouldn't be telling her anything she didn't already know and his attempt at small talk would just make the tension much more palpable than it already is. He reached out to rub the ever-expanding bump under her maternity dress.

"How about some classical on the radio? They say that's good for their development, right? Mozart, Bach, that guy that cut off his ear."

"Van Gogh? He was a painter."

"Of course. What was I saying?" he said in feigned embarrassment. "I meant the deaf guy. The big St. Bernard dog in all those 90 movies."

The phone finally dropped between her legs and she cracked a smile. "Oh, you really know how to impress a lady, don't you?" She leaned forward and played with the AM/FM tuner, finally settling for the second movement of Dvořák's Symphony No. 9th. The slow and soothing build up of woodwinds and strings had a noticeably calming influence.

Colin turned his focus back to the road, giving one last rub to his future son or daughter. "Tonight's going to be good, babe. Your Dad might even whop me in chess again. Any man capable of that has a solid head on him, I say."

Grace turned up the volume and sat back in her seat, eyes closed.

For a moment, he wondered why traffic was so light, but lost his train of thought as a lone bug collided into the windshield. He turned on his wipers, pushed his cruise control to 75 and enjoyed the empty roads ahead.

***

The sun was still out when Colin backed out of his in-law's driveway, a discovery that filled him with relief. These family visits rarely ended so soon, especially when there was a birthday to celebrate. Which was why he was so surprised when Grace had given him the look. Surprised, but happy to oblige.

She mostly reserved the look for social functions, especially those holiday parties at Colin's work that Grace felt obligated to attend for half an hour, possibly longer if the conversation, food and drink were good, but never over an hour. They would arrive, get enough people to see the two of them that their presence was noted, eat and, like clockwork, she would flash the look and Colin would say his goodbyes, coming up with some excuse along the way. They would buy it, all except Dinah of course, who would roll her eyes but otherwise go along with the ruse.

At first, Colin felt no need to say anything, knowing Grace would spill a verbal diary entry as soon as they were alone. Yet as they turned from Pine Street to Gold Avenue, Grace had not uttered a single word. Colin opened his mouth, hesitated and then closed it again. Whatever move he made would be a gamble. Either she would get mad about feeling ignored, or his question would unleash some hidden, emotional beast he would then have to deal with. A minute passed. Maybe more. Grace did not budge from her reclined posture. It was time to diffuse the ticking time bomb. Delicately.

"They really seemed to like your margaritas. You nailed it, babe."

"Dad never touched his," she responded, matter-of-fact. She stared out the side window, eyes fixated on nothing.

"Well... yeah, but he barely touched his burger, either. At that age you really lose your appetite. Not to say he's old. It's just a normal thing... you know? Not drinking much. You should have seen how focused he was on our chess game. My queen never stood a chance after—"

"He's dying, Colin."

"That's not... we don't know that. Even if it is Alzheimer's—"

"It is."

"—that doesn't mean he's... departing us anytime soon. They can have a perfectly normal life for years."

"He didn't remember my name. His own daughter." She looked squarely at him now, her eyes glistening with fresh tears.

The bomb Colin had so delicately worked around was lit. There would be more tears. Much more. Colin reached an arm over her and she fell in the half-embrace, leaning her head on his shoulder and sobbing.

"I should be there for him, especially now. It was cowardly to leave early. But part of me... well, was scared. Scared that I would only remember this version of him, the dad that needs help eating his own birthday cake. The dad who doesn't recognize his own daughter. I don't want that. So, I just sorta... panicked back there and left. It hurt to watch him like that."

Colin, still gripping the wheel with one hand, caressed her soft hair back and forth. They were out of Deming now and heading back north on Route 180. In truth, Colin didn't sympathize at all with what she said. You stuck by your parents, whether they called you Grace, Jimmy Bob, or Rudolph the Red-Nosed Reindeer. His parents, however, were both perfectly healthy, so maybe he wasn't being fair. Maybe.

"Don't beat up yourself, hon. You caught him on a bad day. There will be other times to be there with him."

Grace nodded, wiped her eyes again and looked out her window, seemingly convinced. Colin, however, had serious doubts there would be anything other than "bad days" from here on out. Based on today, his stepfather seemed to be losing his long battle with his own mind and was openly retreating into his own world.

Colin's mind, meanwhile, was at peace, enjoying the quiet of the empty two-lane highway taking them home. This peace would be short-lived. Hours later, Colin would think back often to how they left Deming early and how that one decision set them right in the storm's path. The lurking storm, which sat in hiding, waiting to see what flies got caught in the web.

***

Flashing red brake lights interrupted their evening drive as Colin found himself stuck behind the only other vehicle in miles.

"Unbelievable." He stole a glance at his speedometer, the hand falling to 20 MPH.

"What's this guy thinking?" asked Grace. "It's nothing but empty road ahead."

The vehicle in question, an old Chevy pickup, seemed to crawl, as if the driver was intimidated by something. A graying border collie occupied the truck's bed, barking and yelping at something ahead, yet all Colin could see beyond the truck was empty asphalt stretching to a towering range of desert peaks in the horizon.

"Let's pass, babe," Grace said.

Colin was already halfway in the other lane. He leaned out, accelerated and then stopped. With furrowed brow, he muttered under his breath. "You've got to be kidding me."

91

The Chevy had swerved left, blocking both lanes.

Colin laid on the horn, but the old truck continued its glacial advance.

"Can you squeeze by?" asked Grace.

"Sounds like a death sentence with this guy." Colin rang the horn twice more before the Chevy jerked to the shoulder and stopped.

"Finally," Grace said. "Let's get some distance between us."

Colin had little time to celebrate as a troubling thought swept over him. He looked at the truck he just passed. At first glance, the driver was older, possibly a local rancher. But Colin wasn't focused on the man's tanned, leathery face, or the curled brim cowboy hat he wore. What bothered Colin was the way the man sat hunched over the steering wheel. The man's squinting eyes looked to Colin, or maybe even past Colin. Something was not right.

"We should stop, right?" said Colin. "Check to see if he's ok?" He looked to Grace, she was not looking back, but ahead.

"Pull over," she said in a grave voice.

He did so, a wave of adrenaline forming in his core. Then he saw what had consumed Grace's attention.

A floating pocket of desert dust blocked the road ahead. With each passing second, the tawny cloud thickened and grew as it distorted and swallowed the few fading beams that had penetrated the already overcast sky. The creeping wind pushed east, sucking up heaps of loamy soil from a nearby ranch. Colin let off the gas and, like an open wound, the swelling storm swept past the car and blotted out the dying sun.

"Where the hell did this come from?" said Grace.

"Not a clue." He pulled to a stop on the shoulder of the road and slumped in his seat. "But you know how these dust storms just appear out of nowhere sometimes."

"Well, it sure picked a bad day to surprise us. Can you drive through?"

Colin bit his lip as he looked at the side mirrors. He estimated his visibility was maybe five feet in any direction. But by the time he responded, that range had shrunk considerably. "You know we can't."

"This is just our luck," she said, pulling out her phone. "And of course: No signal. How did we not know there would be a dust storm tonight?"

Colin's gaze fell to the surrounding sea of brown dust, carried by gusts of wind that sounded muted from inside the car. "No clue. I didn't hear anything. It should pass soon, though"

"You think that truck is still back there?"

"I hope so. He'd have to be crazy to drive in these conditions."

The side mirrors were now a solid shade of amber. Colin struggled to see the backside of his own car, let alone the truck they passed. As their conversation died, the couple silently accepted their circumstances as they sat in silence listening to the squalling storm.

"I feel blind," Grace said. "All of New Mexico could be on fire right now and I'd have no idea."

"I'm sure you'd catch on when the car erupted in flames."

"Don't start with me. It was an observation. I —"

"Wait," Colin said, raising his finger to interrupt. "Do you hear that?"

"Hear what?"

Colin leaned toward the windshield and held his breath. Moments before he had heard something; he was sure of it. He forced his brain to ignore the constant cascade of wind outside and heard it again. Intermittent tapping from something hitting the car hood. The tapping grew in frequency and intensity, leaving Colin to speculate rain or light hail. Yet when the source of the drumming sound started colliding with the windshield, Colin could see for himself how wrong he was.

They were insects. Dozens of them, each about an inch long. An elongated, oval-like abdomen connected a pair of wings and six legs. Their head, featuring a prominent pair of antennas, was almost ant like, if not for the curved snout and fang-like beak.

Colin knew next to nothing about bugs, but he recognized these creatures. Masked Hunters. Relatives of the much-maligned assassin bug. A year ago he had found several inside the hospital during a late shift, a discovery that put his fellow nurses in the Geriatrics ward, along with several of the patients, on high alert. The exterminator later found the bedbugs snuggled in the linens of six different beds, resulting in the immediate search for a new laundry service and several embarrassing headlines. Turns out these assassins were notorious for finding their way inside a bedbug infested building to feed.

But that was then. Now, instead of crawling under the beds of elderly patients at work, they were on his windshield, covered in a thick coat of dust and grime that clung to their hard, hairy exteriors like a patch of brown mould.

"What in the hell?" said Colin, as the crablike bugs congregated to cover over half the windshield. He turned on the wipers at full speed. The blades pushed and strained against the growing mass of invertebrates, only clearing a sliver of glass before coming to a stop. The bugs piled on, retaking their lost territory in a matter of seconds.

"Are they attracted to our lights?" said Colin.

"Turn them off then. Turn it all off!"

Colin lunged for the keys and cut the engine, killing the lights. A wave of panic spread in his gut as the hunters continued to scrape and swarm on the glass. His brain skimmed through dozens of hypothetical factoids about the creatures he knew so little about. Were they venomous? Could they break the glass? Would they cling to you like a leech — or like the dirt seemingly glued to them?

The racing thoughts continued, but Colin had no answers other than they were confined to this dark car until either the storm or bugs passed on. Preferably both.

Colin extended a reassuring hand out to the passenger side, eventually finding Grace's back, no more than a dim shadow in the dark car. While he could not see the sky, Colin figured dusk had now officially turned into night. The storm had intercepted any moonlight that could have provided illumination.

He rubbed Grace's back in long, gentle strokes, admiring the soft cotton of the blouse he bought her for their last anniversary. He had always prided himself on taking care of her — being there to listen to her, hug her and comfort her whenever she needed it most. That was his job as a nurse, after all. His solemn duty was to take care of not just Grace, but his community.

But in that moment, Colin had never felt more powerless. More vulnerable. He shuddered as an even worse thought crossed his horizon. Colin was always the more optimistic and upbeat of the couple. If this is what he was thinking, he couldn't imagine the depths where Grace's mind was wandering.

He opened his mouth to say some half-thought that could do something — anything — to reassure Grace, but he was interrupted. He turned to face the windshield. The hive mind swarm was strumming their beaks against the hard ridges of their chests in unison, creating a steady squeaking sound. But Colin was sure what he heard was deeper. More prominent. Angrier.

It rang again from the front of their car, the source now closer. A boundless call from the dirt and dark. It rang like a siren, piercing through glass and steel to the very core of Colin's fear. The frenzied cult of bugs, as if knowing what was about to happen, intensified their screeching, rocking their heads up and down in hysteria.

"What do we do?" cried Grace.

Before he could answer, the weakened windshield announced its resignation, forming narrow fissures across the glass. The sound reminded Colin of the surface of a frozen lake cracking open after a wrong step on the ice. A few of the bugs somehow squeezed through the small gaps. Barbed, hairy legs crawled across his face. The glass was straining under the pressure. Any second and it would shatter completely. He waved the intruders off. He could hear Grace's muted shouts, a mere whisper compared to the deafening combination of wind and thousands of flailing wings.

"Drive! Colin, drive!" she screeched.

Half-blind, Colin reached for the ignition, powering on the not-so-empty car and stepped on the gas. He could feel some of the claw-like legs dig further in his face, despite the rush of grit and earth clearing through the moving car. Colin had no idea In what direction they were moving. The car laboured against some unseen obstruction, its old tires climbing over and then crushing what could only be masses of bugs on the asphalt. He accelerated, not worrying if he was on the road or dirt, until a collision sent him flying forward into the airbag.

Colin's eyes opened to the deflated airbag smothered with the collective mess of several flattened hunters. He wiped a thick glop of guts off his face and turned to do the same to Grace. She was conscious, but dazed, locked in a state of shock that Colin wasn't sure he could get her out of. A thin stream of blood fell from her hairline.

"Grace, honey, listen to me." He swatted away the incoming wave of fresh hunters. "Don't open your eyes and keep your mouth covered. These things seem to —"

"I'm bit," Grace mumbled, her matter-of-fact tone surprising Colin. He of course had noticed the oozing red sores on his girlfriend's face and imagined his own face was not a pretty sight. He had felt the countless piercing bites during the initial breakthrough, the pain comparable to a bee sting or a shot at the doctor's office. But the hunters' ability to bite was far from his mind. His thoughts dwelled on something much worse.

"I know it hurts. I need you to do what I say. We need to leave the car, we're not safe here."

"But—"

"We're not safe here, Grace! Please. Keep one hand on me and the other over your face. Don't let them get close to your eyes."

Grace nodded, regaining her perspective of the situation. Colin unbuckled his seatbelt, said a silent prayer and opened the door.

He shielded his eyes from dirt and bugs and hunched to stay low, circling around the back of his wrecked car. He opened the passenger side door and felt Grace's warm, damp hand. She grasped him and stepped out into the whirlwind.

He edged forward, unable to see or feel with both hands occupied. He collided with the cold steel of what he could only assume was the object they crashed into. It was the truck they had passed earlier. He opened his eyes for a second, hoping to sense the movements of the Border Collie and its elderly owner, but the truck was abandoned, overtaken by a colony of hunters who used the old Chevy as a temporary pit stop before flying off and disappearing into the brown haze. He gripped the protruding passenger side mirror, found the door and yanked at the silver handle repeatedly. It didn't open.

A surge of dread overcame him as he realized what that meant. The truck was the only other car they saw on the road before the storm hit and not only was it locked, but the old man and his dog had run off. He and Grace were now officially on their own. His desperation escalating, Colin raised a clenched fist, riddled with red sores, to shatter the window before coming to his senses and realizing just what that would do to their only potential shelter.

For a moment, he did nothing. Said nothing. His thoughts ricocheted between retreating to their car or going after the old man. Grace seemed to drift into a half-conscious state of stupor, still clinging to his hand and Colin shocked himself at a sudden feeling of jealousy. Grace was in no shape to go ten feet. And while a part of him acknowledged the possibility of leaving her behind while he ventured off to chase down the keys to the truck, another part of him violently disagreed with the cowardly move of leaving the love of his life behind to perish. His confidence in his own ability to find the driver was shaky at best, but to find the driver and return before the hunters and elements overtook Grace seemed like a near certain impossibility. He knew he was utterly alone except for her company, but as the seconds ticked by, the lack of an alternative plan grew more and more apparent.

He opened his eyes again to face Grace, leaning slightly to press his forehead against hers. He wiped away a trickle of blood falling past her ear and made the most difficult decision he would ever face.

"Grace... I love you more —"

"No," she interrupted, shaking her head.

"I need to find those keys. You are safest under the—"

She kept shaking her head, a small stream of tears falling despite how dry her eyes must be.

"Under the truck, Grace. If you stay flat and keep your shirt over your face, they can't get to you. It won't be for long."

After a moment of continued protest she relented, giving him a kiss and a final warning to stay safe before becoming prone under the truck. Colin gave one last look at Grace and departed, removing his outer shirt and tying it like a bandana to cover his nose and mouth.

He walked on with his head down. Visibility was poor, maybe three feet at most. He could barely see the charcoal asphalt of the road below. Some hunters crawled along his moving feet, but most were still scurrying above his head. Colin arched his neck and kept his eyes to the ground, so that most of the dust and bugs flew into his forehead and scalp rather than the face. He had no idea where the man had gone. Did the dog run off when the storm started? Where would the dog have gone?

He followed the road southeast, keeping to the shoulder in case any reckless drivers tried to drive through the mess. If there were others, he certainly wouldn't hear them coming over the buzzing hunters. Their droning seemed to overpower all other sounds and Colin struggled to even focus enough to hear his own inner thoughts.

A flash of light pierced through the thick dust. Colin saw it fleetingly from the corner of his eye. He stepped off the shoulder to investigate and felt the hairs on his neck rise as a current of static energy passed through him. He followed the faint flashes. Something sharp dug into his leg. He slapped his hand down to get at the stinging hunter, but felt the clatter of cold steel. He had walked straight into the barbed wire fencing separating the highway from the neighbouring pastures. Colin winced as the countless bites, scrapes and cuts his body had become numb to suddenly made themselves known. He could feel damp patches in his jeans as blood trickled down.

In an instant, his world lit up as a blue blaze leapt from the barbed fencing before him. His body jolted away in a reaction of pure instinct. He regained his footing and looked back at the fence which was still emitting small blue flames from a dizzying build-up of static energy.

Colin thought back to the gray collie he saw briefly and pondered. Like its owner, the dog was older. Too old to make the jump, let alone see the fence through the haze. He turned his back to the light show and returned to the shoulder.

He continued southeast and stumbled upon a T intersection. A brown metal sign greeted him on the corner of the intersection. He raised a hand to clear a heap of dust from the sign to reveal City of Rocks State Park and an arrow pointing right.

There was a faint glimmer of hope. Pure speculative hope as he considered the possibility. He knew City of Rocks of course from his countless trips down the highway. In fact, he had taken Grace there years earlier for an overnight camping trip. Over there, gigantic rock formations sprouted from the ground like weeds. Any native of the area would know the potential shelter from the elements the volcanic rocks could provide.

Without waiting, he turned right, forgetting momentarily to keep his head down as more hunters converged around him, following him either due to his scent or just to keep eyes on the wandering intruder who changed his path.

It was a five-mile trek, but with the raging wind to his back, he made good time. At least he thought he did. Time didn't seem continuous to Colin and his recognition of progress happened like pictures in a photo reel: fixed stages of consciousness speckled between the numbing sensation of being engulfed by that sweeping sea of brown nothingness. In his mind, he was still with Grace, huddling under the rusted undercarriage of the old Chevy. That is until an occasional sting from a passing Hunter tore him out of the illusion.

This continued until he felt the asphalt turn to dirt beneath his weary feet. He lifted his head to gaze at several silhouettes towering over him. He had arrived at City of Rocks, the rocky labyrinth. As expected, the haze shrouded the protruding rock columns. He ventured further into the maze-like geological formation, following pockets of grass and shrubs that formed a natural trailhead through the hundreds of otherworldly sculptures.

Hunters continued to stalk Colin from the skies. He could not guess how many thousands of them were beyond his limited vision, but their shrill cries had lost some of its intensity. A good omen, perhaps, he hoped.

And in that waning moment, Colin realized. for the first time since leaving Grace, he could hear something other than the hunters. It was faint at first. He closed his eyes to focus, waiting to see if his ears, no doubt suffering from sensory overload, deceived him.

He heard it twice, enough to make up his mind. He moved toward the voice.

He cut through the middle of the park first, his confidence growing as the calls grew clearer. Ahead was a series of broad boulders that converged and collapsed against each other to form a natural barricade. Colin had no desire to detour. He found the shortest of the bunch and climbed to the top — a decision that resulted in immediate regret.

Hunters swarmed to his new heightened position. The bugs that were so hesitant to swoop down and attack him below the rocks were now engaged in a free for all. Colin jumped on the other side of the barricade, wiping away two hunters that had fathered by his eyes. Why the eyes? he thought, despite his growing certainty that he already knew the unfortunate answer.

He knew it back when they first broke through the windshield. They went straight for his eyes, the most moisture-rich part of the face other than the mouth. Colin didn't have the heart, or the time, to tell Grace why she had to cover her eyes and mouth. She had been on the brink of shutting down completely from the blood loss. God, make sure she keeps her eyes covered. Keep her under that car, he prayed.

Even now, he felt his burning eyes grow drier. He licked his lips, careful not to open his mouth too wide. Colin didn't know of any bugs that willingly fly kamikaze right into an open mouth, only to suck up every ounce of moisture. Yet Colin knew the frantic hunters surrounding him were a scientific anomaly. Possibly a subspecies of the ordinary hunters he encountered in the hospital last year. There was something alien about their ability to move, think and act collectively.

A human cry pierced the ear, jolting Colin back to his search. the dirt path grew narrower, forcing a tight squeeze in between two rocky pinnacles, under the reaching branches of a charred black tree and into a small clearing, where Colin came to a full stop.

Despite his limited vision, he was sure he had seen silhouettes standing on one of the tall rocks he passed, looking down at him. He turned back to investigate and met a burst of dirty wind, nearly knocking him to the ground. Not wasting a second, the hunters dove on their prey. Colin stayed low, crawling to the cover of nearby rocks.

The powerful surge of wind receded, allowing a brief window of time for Colin to catch his breath and take in his surroundings. He counted to three and resumed his sprint toward the wailing voice. He was for sure noticed by the travelling hive mind, but he didn't look back. The cry turned into audible words.

"Gunter! Gunter!" the voice repeated in a full throat yell.

Colin cleared another row of boulders and nearly ran into the crying man.

He sat on a bench, head down, shouting at his dirty leather boots. The rancher, who Colin last saw hunched over his steering wheel a few hours ago, was dying. Colin was sure of it. Oozing cuts riddled the man's leathery face. The hat Colin noticed earlier was missing, a balding, reddened head in its place. He wore a suit of shifting hunters, feeding on their new host. His cries for Gunter continued, each new gasp allowing several hunters to travel in and out of his open mouth like a highway tunnel. Colin didn't see the man swatting, spitting, or fighting back. He had simply... given up.

Colin closed the small gap between them, removing the crumpled shirt that had served as an impromptu mask and brought it to the rancher's face.

"Cover your eyes and mouth!" The man didn't react and in seconds hunters started crawling on Colin's extended arm and on his torso.

"Take the shirt!" Colin repeated, raising his voice over the shrieks of the hunters.

"Gunter. Did you see him?" the man asked before coughing out a glob of bugs and blood onto Colin's shirt.

"No," Colin said, wincing as he felt the familiar sting on the back of his neck. He used his free hand to wipe the neck clear, picking up some of his own blood. The man had still not taken his shirt. "I'm sorry, but I need your keys. My pregnant wife—"

"They killed my damn dog."

"Look, I can take you back with us. Your windows are still intact. I just need the keys."

"They killed Gunter."

The man lowered his head, hitting Colin's wrist, causing the shirt to drop to the dirt. It writhed and wormed as several hunters dragged the fabric across the desert floor. Colin put a foot down, hearing a satisfying crunch. He picked up the shirt, looked at the mess and groaned. He couldn't waste any more time. Grace was still out there.

"If you don't want to save yourself, at least help me out. My child is in that woman and I'm leaving here, either with you, or just your keys."

The man let out a pitiful chuckle. As if waiting for their opportunity, several more hunters flew into the open mouth and eyes. He erupted in a coughing fit. "Look at me. LOOK at me!" Colin did and saw most of his face now covered. A squadron of burrowing bugs started excavating his eyes. "It's over. For everyone. Any second now and I'll be opening a cold one in heaven. Maybe I'll have a porch. Gunter always liked those roundabout ones."

Colin grasped the coughing man and shook. "Don't give up! You have keys. What do you not understand about that!" His hand moved instinctively to the old rancher's face, but the hunters wouldn't budge, as if they had connected with each other, creating an impenetrable barrier. More flocked to the two and Colin leaped back.

The old rancher laughed again. Then his face went neutral, as if his closed eyes were studying the distant horizon. "No. Not him." His face was pure fear now. "I won't look at that face. It ain't human!"

"Who?" Colin asked from a safe distance. The bloodied shirt had returned to cover his lower face.

"Him! The one following me. He killed Gunter, he kill—"

More coughing. Colin had never heard such a terrible sound coming from any person, even at the hospital. Hunters swarmed and swarmed, covering every square inch of the man until the coughing suddenly stopped.

Colin ran toward the commotion. He didn't check for a pulse. He cleared the hunters covering the man's left side pocket and dug in. Nothing. He could feel the things crawling up and down his back. He reached over the dead man's lap and cleared the other pocket. A few hunters squirmed inside, but also something metal, slightly cold to the touch. The keys jingled as he pulled them out. He ran, not daring to look back for a second.

For a moment, he swore he heard something heavy being dragged across the dirt.

***

Grace, still lying prone, thought she was only imagining the gruff panting sounds. She was going crazy, after all. Hiding from nightmare creatures under an abandoned truck certainly made her feel crazy. As the gruff panting grew closer, she uncovered her face to peek at the thing just outside the truck.

It was a dog, the Border Collie they had spotted earlier, returning to his owner's truck. The dog slowed, lowered its snout, then hesitantly started sniffing, as if it could almost catch her scent under all the dusty blustery air. She froze, afraid to adjust her position, but not sure why the canine company drove such panic through her. She had no problems with dogs; she had grown up with several. Yet this dog, with its stiff movements and grungy gray and white coat, was just strange enough for Grace to stay in place, hidden away. Now that she was looking at the thing, didn't its fur appear to be moving? Flowing in little waves? Not just in the same direction either, for if that were the case, the culprit would obviously be the wind. No, this dog's fur was shuddering. No, not its fur, Grace realized. Something underneath the fur.

109

The bugs appeared then, like hidden lice springing from the scalp to find new skin. They crawled up and down the suddenly congested freeway, the dog's legs.

Grace buried her face back in her shirt, waiting for the thing to move on, to find its owner, get lost in the desert, anything but stay there with her. Unfortunately, none of these things happened.

She heard the dog's vicious growling, she thought of her husband, out there in the dust somewhere. Possibly dead. And in the slim chance he was alive, just where the hell was he?

With shaking hands, she once again lowered her face covering and looked into the angry, yellow eyes of a creature that at some point recently stopped being a dog and become something entirely different. It snarled at her, lowering its front half and bending its forepaws to form an attack position.

She once again wondered just—

***

—where the hell am I, Colin thought. He was lost and had been for some time. The dust had not let up at all since he left City of Rocks. In fact, the brown aura was thicker now than ever before. After initially running back, his pace had slowed to a crawl as exhaustion swept through his lungs, heart and legs. Worse, Colin was now going against the wind. A useful tool for confirming he is in fact heading southwest—assuming the wind didn't

110

change direction—but otherwise an overall nuisance that made his already slow pace even more sluggish.

Another curiosity was the lack of hunters. He had crossed paths with a few small cohorts, but since taking the dead man's keys, they had been sparse. He sensed they had somewhere else to be within the vast brown haze.

Not that Colin felt alone. Far from it. As he trekked clumsily along with his neck bent, head down and face covered in ragged clothing, like a drunken hobo idling around town, he had felt small tremors from under his feet, strong enough to shake off some of the accumulated dirt from weeds and yuccas. It was an undeniable sensation that something other than bugs, something far larger, crept nearby, marched just out of sight. One quake was so intense, Colin had wondered if the force was coming from underground, as if some creature was tunneling its way around.

He thought of running again. Half a minute could make all the difference, depending on how bad Grace was. Any more tremors would convince his tired mind that the ground was caving in, potentially trapping him with whatever was digging below. But his burning lungs and jelly legs objected.

With each passing minute, Colin hoped to feel the dirt turn to asphalt beneath his feet. Surely he was getting close now. Yet, having passed no recognizable landmarks, there was no way to know

111

for sure. The wind must have shifted at some point, urging him off course. Startled by his own incompetence, a wave of adrenaline surged through him. The energy that comes through sheer anger and curled fists, pumping his legs back to a jog.

She's not dead. Not dead. Not yet. He churned these hopes in his head, but with every repeat of the mantra, he doubted the thoughts even more. A dry, winding streambed formed beneath him and he followed it, picking up his pace until he felt mud, then shallow water. He moved alongside it, refusing to let off the gas, refusing to acknowledge his burning lungs and his hundred-pound thighs weighing him down, until all it once, he stopped cold.

A figure stood ahead, not ten feet from Colin's trembling legs.

The thing floated toward Colin, carried by a gust of howling wind. Colin drew closer himself.

"Grace! Is that you?"

Whoever it was didn't speak, but continued advancing. In one sudden strike of comprehension, Colin could see it was not Grace. It was the shape of someone tall, at least eight feet. There was no visible skin or face. Its outline simply blended in the dust, as if it were part of the dust storm and made of grit and sand itself, but combined to have a fixed form.

The fact that the silhouette was almost completely featureless only intensified Colin's fear—an alien fear that ate on his very sense of being. A fear that his brain was too slow to process the figure and only seeing a 2D image of something whose authentic form was beyond the capacity of even 3D vision.

In this fear, mental self-preservation kicked in and Colin forced himself to imagine some face. A pair of eyes, a mouth perhaps. Anything to add some level of understanding to the loosely packed dust cloud that just happened to be shaped like the tallest man on record.

It whispered a single word that carried effortlessly. A single word that the wind and chaos should have drowned out, yet was perfectly clear to Colin. So clear he heard it inside his head.

"Deeadd."

Satisfied, the sooty phantom collapsed back to thousands of individual particles of dirt. Its essence poured back into the storm.

Colin stood paralyzed, trying to process what was clearly a hallucination or dream, for he had no other justifiable explanations in his head for what he just witnessed. He had to wake up, clear his head, cool off. He was far too hot, a fact that he was only distantly aware of until now. Dirt clung to his sweaty skin. His legs burned.

Why am I just feeling this now? What is wrong with me?

He looked down and saw exactly what was wrong.

Colin was standing in a small pool of greenish water about five feet across. He was literally in hot water and he had walked right into it unknowingly while under the phantom's trance.

He knew there were hot springs between City of Rocks and route 180. The collection of geothermal pools had long attracted campers, loungers and bored tourists. Instead of finding relief in the comfort that he finally knew where he was in proximity to the road, Colin's mind weighed heavy with a whispered proclamation that had taken root. He had no strength to deny its claim. Grace was

(deeadd)

gone. He had been too late and she had been in bad enough shape when he left, an event that to Colin felt days old. He had failed his own wife and unborn child.

This acknowledgment of fault, of failure, seemed to wipe his mind clean and he felt free of responsibility. It was the key to unlock that burdensome ball and chain he dragged across the desert. He had tried and now his muscles needed rest. They needed, no, deserved, a good long soak. Why else would fate lead him here, of all places?

He let go, collapsing into the steaming, sulfuric smelling water, which had turned into an impromptu mud bath with all the dirt. Colin didn't mind. He felt he could die here and now, regret free. After all, did he not have silent doubts the baby was even his? Especially the way Grace could drink herself into situations. Sure, he had repressed his initial impulse, but part of him still remembered stiffening up when he first saw the two pink lines on the pregnancy test. And if she were somehow holding on still, wouldn't it be cruel to keep her alive? Keep her in pain?

Colin sunk further, submerging his head in the steamy springs. And if he somehow survived this and managed to find the truck and drive to safety, would he not still have Dinah? The same woman who understood just how Grace could be and who never hesitated to share her own musings on how she could never find the right guy for her, all while looking at him with those wide, eager eyes and her not-so-subtle looks? And was there not one night three months back, where he comforted Dinah after their hack-of-a-supervisor berated her for nothing and after work, he had sent a text to Grace, apologizing that he got stuck with a sudden graveyard shift and wouldn't be home that night? And did he not constantly crave Dinah's warm embrace, even long after that one spontaneous night?

He felt his blood being deprived of oxygen. Yes, he needed air, but the air up there was bad, heavy with

(guilt)

grit. It was far nicer down here, away from the storm. It seemed right down here. If he was dying, then it was a fine way to go out, he figured. After all—

Some reflex kicked in and his mouth gaped open as if had a great yawn. Muddy gook flooded in, tasting of rotten eggs. The taste woke him free

115

of his suicidal spell and he lunged out of the springs, gasping and wheezing dry, dirty air.

What the HELL were you thinking! She's alive and you're a coward. MAN UP, Colin!

He ran, dripping hot water behind him, leather loafers squishing with each step. His interior compass was back and while he could still not see through the dust, he navigated through it without the overbearing physical slog. He could not afford to go at his prior pace. He had lost time to make up, after all.

Tunnel vision had set in and he did not immediately notice the return of the insectile hive. They had appeared so suddenly, with such accurate precision, convincing Colin that they were never that far away at all. They had been stalking him in the storm's cover, not making their presence known until Colin's second wind left them no other choice. They coated his wet clothing, biting and bruising with an aggression Colin had not seen before.

The pain, along with his conscience, was back with a vengeance. He wanted to scream, to swat, to make his utter agony known to the hunters. He wanted to fight back and show he would not simply ignore what they were doing to him. What they were doing to Grace. But he knew this would only allow the mass of bugs to surround and shackle him up, slowing his momentum.

Bite me all you want. I'm WINNING.

They went for his eyes, trying to suck out any moisture. But that was their modus operandi and

Colin was prepared. His instincts were sharp and he snapped his ragged shirt at any advancers like a rowdy teenage boy in the locker room. He swept away the few that breached his defenses with a quick wipe across the face. But there were more. Always more.

"Deeeaadd," a familiar, raspy voice whispered again. The loamy apparition had reappeared dead ahead. Colin did not dare to stop. He accelerated, ready to ram the thing.

Or hopefully run right through it.

It was prepared for this and, like a high-powered magnet, it drew hunters to itself—maybe a hundred in the time it took Colin to blink in reaction. They attached effortlessly to its limbs, then torso, then face, creating the illusion of the thing being sketched in real time. Brought to life by the hunters that stuck to it like a chemical bond.

The bug covered creature grasped for Colin's throat. Its hard shell of a hand squeezed tight around Colin's windpipe with such force he felt like his neck might just snap. The other hand ripped Colin's old shirt from his face, tearing it in two as if the cotton were just a sheet of paper. Hunters crawled up to Colin's newly exposed face, digging their hairy, barbed limbs into his cheeks, lips and nose, blocking the precious intake of air. He would pass out soon, either from lack of oxygen or a broken neck. He shut his eyes just as hunters assaulted his eyelids. It was a sharp pain, the pain of being poked and stabbed by needles.

"DEEAAADD!"

Ignoring the pain, Colin reached blindly in his pocket for his phone. His fingers caressed the metallic corners until he felt the raised power button. He pressed down and turned the lit screen toward his face. The light, dim as it was, caused the hunters to retreat toward the sides and back of his head. Colin opened his eyelids to a thin squint. He poked at his settings, but his world was spinning and he hit his news app instead. The stranglehold was growing tighter, the yellow, orange and brown colors of the bug-ridden storm fading to gray. He poked his screen again and finally saw it. His last shot at survival. His shaking index finger crashed against the phone so hard he jammed the finger. Despite the pain, he had hit his target.

The phone's flashlight beamed at full brightness. A swarm of hunters extended their wings and fled away from the mobile beacon, including those responsible for the lobster-like grip on his throat. He waved the light, bringing it up close to the creature and the remaining hunters flung back in reaction. The creature was once again a formless shadow, naked without its hairy, thick shell and Colin broke free in a sprint, not daring to look back.

He felt the thud of asphalt below his feet. He was back on the road at long last. He took a sharp turn and ran up the road.

Please be alive. Oh GOD, please be alive, Grace. Hang in there and I swear I'll never abandon you again. I—

His shoes squished on something soft in the road, cutting his prayer short. His heart skipped a beat as he looked down.

It was the old man's Border Collie. Bloodied and coated in flattened hunters. Its head hung limp. Colin lifted it and confirmed the cause of death. Broken neck. He wondered if the dog attacked Grace and if so, how many more injuries did she sustain? He felt an urge to stomp the dead dog, but heard the oncoming wave of hunters behind him.

The next moment, Colin stumbled into the back of the truck. He hugged the cold steel, said a silent prayer and got to his knees, calling for his wife.

There was no response. No human response, at least. Instead, the buzzing ensemble of hunters greeted their crouching guest. The hunters were crawling over Grace, who was still and silent on the asphalt.

"NOOO, GRACE!"

Colin pulled her out, brushing off the guilty hunters in hurried, gentle swipes. He dug out the keys. The rancher's truck was old. He would have to manually unlock the car to get in. He lifted Grace to her feet and hugged her close around the waist, then stuck the key in and turned until he heard the satisfying click as the knob inside shot up. A few hunters circled above, but not enough to break the truck's window shield. Not yet, at least. But Colin had little doubt the roaring wind was masking the sound of millions of the dust-covered hunters. They were coming all right, and once the car powered on, they would stick out like a sore thumb.

Colin knew the only path to survival was to out-stealth the assassin bugs.

He lifted Grace up to the passenger seat, then slammed the door and circled to the truck bed.

Thanks for the lift, but I hope you kept more than your dog back here.

Colin hopped on the bed and fumbled through a rusty toolbox. He pulled out a tire iron, then threw the box aside, uncovering a red two-gallon can of gas about half full. Colin took it, then smashed the truck's brake lights with the tire iron. Glass shattered and, to Colin's delight, the old truck's alarm stayed silent.

He circled around to the driver's side, flung the gas and iron aside and rushed to Grace, who remained slumped back and unconscious. Her face was raw with fresh sores, bites and bruises. He placed two fingers on her throat. He waited and waited. Time moved at a glacier pace.

In a moment of pure elation, Colin felt the faint beat of her heart—weak, but a pulse, nevertheless. She was alive, his Grace was alive!

"I'm here now," he said while caressing her and removing dead hunters from her tangled, greasy hair.

Her bloodshot eyes opened. "Colin?"

"I'm here, Grace. Are you in any pain?"

Of course she is, you idiot. You're in pain. She's in pain. Anyone would be in pain after what happened.

She opened her mouth—not to speak, but to breathe.

Her hyperventilating wasn't what concerned Colin. Neither was her sporadic heart rate. No, what turned Colin's blood cold was the scratchy crunch he heard with each heartbeat. He had heard it many times at the Hospital and it was never pleasant. Her lung had collapsed. And there was nothing he could do other than calm her down. She would need medical treatment to get rid of the excess air in her lungs.

Suddenly Grace erupted in a fit of coughs. Her face turned nearly as red as her faded lipstick as she continued to hack away until finally, she coughed up a brown, wet chunk of something soft which fell onto the floor of the truck. It was dirt, a whole handful of it. Something stirred in the muddy mess and without thinking, Colin stomped it with three forceful drops of his boot. He spotted at least three dead hunters in the aftermath, but did all he could to stay stoic for Grace.

Holy God, she had those things in her. INSIDE. But if I panic, she panics.

"Ok, Grace. Don't panic. We're safe here. Breathe in, deep and slow. Breathe in... breathe out."

He continued until Grace mimicked his controlled breathing exercise.

"Good, babe. Keep doing that. The bugs don't know we're here. If we keep our lights off, we can drive this car out of here. I just need you to stay quiet, okay?"

She nodded drunkenly while slipping off into her own world.

Colin bit the inside of his cheeks. He had no earthy idea whether the bugs and whatever else was out there, knew they were here. That didn't matter. Grace believed him.

"I love you, Grace. Now let's get the hell out of here."

After double checking that he had disabled both the high and low beams, he put the truck in drive, praying his batting practice took care of the taillights. They crept along in utter silence, driving through the dust. But to Colin, the storm seemed infinite and impenetrable. Twice the truck's front tires swerved off the road, both times Colin readjusted and found pavement. Grace fell in and out of consciousness and Colin left her alone, too scared to make any sound beyond the low hum of the engine. His plan was working. They were sneaking out undetected into the storm. There was hope and plenty of it. Colin imagined the dust thinning, blown away by that eternal law of nature that always sought to return to normalcy. Perhaps there was no imagination involved, for Colin thought he could see two car lengths ahead of him, a feat that would have been impossible mere minutes ago.

Grace shook in her seat, half-awake. Her formally blue eyes were now a pale gray, as if those things had sucked all the melanin from her irises. In a dim, wheezy voice, she whispered. "Is he still there?"

"The rancher, you mean? He died, Grace, I tried—"

"No... not him. The... the bug man."

Colin's hands fell from the wheel like rocks in water and he quickly lifted them back. They felt heavy. So heavy. "Grace, what did you see?"

She opened her mouth to answer, but coughed up another lump of dirt.

Colin took one of her hands. "Never mind. Just focus on your breathing, babe. We can worry about everything else later."

But Colin did worry. He worried that he already knew exactly who this "bug man" was and his hallucination back at the hot springs was anything but a hallucination. And if this "bug man" was out there, where was it now? He put more pressure on the gas. The wheels turned and turned, slowly pulling them out of this hellish nightmare. The dust continued to dissipate and soon, pockets of night sky formed on the horizon, morphing and growing until he could make out individual stars. They surely were at the edge of the storm. Any second now and they would see everything. He would never take vision for granted again.

And then he did see something. Road— unobstructed and endless just as a New Mexico

123

highway should be—stretching alongside prickly pears and yuccas and just beyond, the shy luminous moon, peeking behind gray puffy storm clouds.

And something else. Something blocking the gateway to this bright, natural, and comfortable world.

At the threshold, where the dust was light and lazy stood a giant, covered from head to toe in writhing, hungry hunters. It had found them.

Colin rammed on the gas, unwavering, even as the storm carried dust and hunters to block out those patches of beautiful horizon that now were as distant as a dream. That intelligent, surging hive mind encircled the old Chevy, closing in on their desperate, frightened target until the strained truck could not move an inch further against the growing organic mass called to action by that lurking being.

He grasped for his phone, but it still had no signal. Its power bar was nothing but a thin red line, reading five percent. Then four percent. With such little time he gave in to impulse. He would rather die as an active fool than die doing nothing. He enabled the phone's flashlight yet again, rolled the window down halfway and heaved, doing his best impression of Cy Young. Hunters flew through the open window and he pulled himself up as high as he could. They flew into his chest, angry and desperate as a gang of summer hornets. But Colin's fingers were already on the button and the gap in the window shrunk until nothing remained. Ignoring the few hunters that made it in, Colin stared out the window, wild-eyed. He wore the expression of a five-year-old waiting to see if Mom brought home a tub of Rocky Road from the store.

Amazingly, the phone had landed screen up, a small, somber searchlight advertising its message that technically this is light, which you hate because for some reason you hate all things that are good, so fly away now, fly away or you'll get some more, you hear?

That light, which had taken on all Colin's desperate energy, never stood a chance. Hundreds of hunters suffocated the phone, their embrace killing the short-lived broadcast that was but a mere nuisance against their strength of numbers.

Colin's heart sank to his intestines. They were out of options. There was no plausible scenario both of them would live to see another day. Grace was wide awake now; eyes glued open in primal fear. He looked to her, then at her, at his unborn child.

They will live, so help me God.

His cards were on the table. Evil had the better hand. But there was another player, wasn't there? The ultimate player. Fate.

Elements clicked into place. The truck. The gas can he found. If this were really fate, the rancher would have been a smoker. He opened the glove compartment and sure enough found himself with a box of 20 strike matches, the branding faded except for the faint image of a single red cartoon flame.

Grace looked at Colin, then the matchbox he relentlessly studied, then the can of gas. Colin didn't need to explain what he was about to do. Her look of disturbed fury told him she knew enough.

"DON'T YOU DARE!"

"When I leave—"

"Shut up!"

"I want you to count to thirty seconds—"

"Just SHUT UP! I WON'T LET YOU."

"And drive. Don't look back, just get out of here."

"Don't you see I need you? We need you!"

The crack had reached three corners of the windshield now. It looked like an intricate spiderweb.

Colin forced a smile, leaned in and kissed her belly. "I love you, Grace. I always have." He removed a match, pocketed it and grasped the gas. "If it's a boy, name it after your dad. Walt has a nice ring to it."

There was another shrill crack. Before she could protest further, Colin barreled out, slamming the door to the sound of his wife's sobs. He shoved past waves of hunters, no longer concerned with covering his face. Their squeaky strumming was now louder than ever before. It was open season and they swarmed toward his eyes, hungry and eager. He doused his hand with the potent smelling fluid, struck a match and let it ignite. His hand caught immediately. The scalding pain seemed to consume his skin and stab at his nerves. But an armada of kamikaze hunters dove into the blaze and extinguished it, leaving nothing but Colin's hand, raw and scorched. He shrieked, partly from the pain, but mostly from the nearby truck still idling indecisively. Her name formed in his throat and he wanted nothing more than to curse her out. He could have just lost a hand, then run for his life on foot. Now there were no other options. No more half-measures.

He emptied the can over his shirt, jeans and head. His soaking mop of hair leaked gas and he thought he could actually sense the hesitation in the hunters that got soaked with him. The lurker must have sensed the same thing, for it and its writhing, moving shell was racing toward Colin at full charge. He struck a second match and roared.

"THIS IS FOR MY KID! SO BUZZ OFF YOU CREEP OR BURN IN HELL LIKE YOUR FRIENDS!"

He didn't even need to drop the match this time. Colin's world ignited in wild, dancing flames. There was incredible pain as the wildfire burned through his skin and reached his nerves. Hunters scrambled wildly like nightmare fireflies, their circuits overheated and scrambled. He turned to the Chevy. It was still there, still unmoving in the fishbowl of earth, wind and fire. Colin's mind reached past the agony to something even more painful. Oh, God, what if she doesn't leave? She was clearly in shock, and I killed myself for nothing. We'll both die out here.

Then the truck roared to life, pulled forward, jerked to a stop, then drove out of sight. Out of mind. Darkness came, but not death. The fire ate greedily, making its way through his scorched skin.

He writhed on the road like a dying worm, convinced that some vehicle would appear out of nowhere and flatten him to a pancake. He dragged and twisted his weight forward, his muscles screaming at him, until he felt soft earth underneath him and collapsed into its dirty embrace. Pin needle holes opened up around him and expanded, letting loose great swaths of soil until a storm of hunters vomited out like some monstrous birthing canal. He wanted to shout, but no sound left his mouth. For all he knew, the flames had burned his own vocal cords to nothing.

Colin pleaded for death, but his body stubbornly held on as hunters feasted, digging into his eyes, turning them into dark craters. There was no more pain. Just the sensation of being extinguished. Of being depleted. And then, when they finished, Colin felt something entirely different. A tingle crept over him as the hunters regurgitated some god-forsaken moisturizer that coated him from head to toe. The warm sticky goop reminded him of Old Ruthie, his childhood Golden Retriever and her wet, sloppy kisses on those hot Texas summers way back when. He took refuge in this warm nostalgia, taking in the aroma of hidden blackberry stashes and his uncle's livestock. And that is where his mind stayed.

And maybe, just maybe, his lack of vision was a blessing. Besides, he was being dragged now. Dragged down into an unseen nether world beneath the bedrock. Soon, he would join the lurker, its host of hunters, the Old Rancher and whoever else they brought down here and that was something he felt comfortable leaving to his imagination.

A Dark Day
Philip J. Thomas

Josh Capra followed the young woman closely as she approached the Bacchus wine-tasting pavilion. He'd been on her trail for over ten minutes, keeping a safe distance and nosing through the desolate pathways of the Renaissance Faire. He wasn't a killer by nature, but that didn't matter on this particular day. After a tight intake of breath, he palmed the blood-flecked handle of the four-inch butter knife in his pocket. He had stolen it several hours earlier from the Nachos of Nottingham food stand; it had proved to be an easily concealable instrument of death.

The visibly inebriated woman sat on a stool around the nest of bodies costumed as court jesters and voluptuous wenches. She was accompanied by another female who asked for two samples of Knight's Reward, an unusually dry, popular wine at the festival. Josh knew the scenario wasn't going to work. With so many potential witnesses, someone was sure to notice him retrieve the blade and puncture her spine. But he couldn't give up now.

The body count was rising... and she was last on his list.

***

When Josh woke that morning, the last thing on his mind was murder. He had thoughts of sipping honey mead, devouring ham on a bone, attending the Ultimate Horse Joust and spending the day wandering the annual Pennsylvania Renaissance Faire with his fiancée, Barbara and their two friends.

It was something they did every year since working together at the Shake Shack, where they'd all met. That was twelve years ago. Now in their thirties, they'd all transitioned to other careers, graduated from college, got on with their lives. But this was the one thing that brought them together every October no matter what life told them. They never missed it. And this year was no different.

It was Greg's turn as the designated driver, so he was tasked with picking up Sharanda and Barb before finally scooping up Josh. He wasn't thrilled about it, getting to watch his friends tag down wine and mead and ale all afternoon with him relegated to the soda stand, but that was how it went. Last year it had been Barbara's turn, the year before, it was Josh's. Greg knew his turn was coming, but it didn't make it sting any less.

After their hour-and-a-half drive from Philadelphia and a stop at a rest area for McDonald's breakfast, they arrived at a row of sedans and SUVs, snaking their way through the parking lot. The Renaissance Faire sign welcomed them. An arrow pointed to the entrance. But they didn't need directions because Josh Capra, Barbara

131

Connelly, Sharanda Owens and Greg Russo knew the place probably better than anyone who worked there.

They found a parking spot in the far left of the lot and sloshed their way through the soggy grass to the front gate. "I have to use the latrine," Barbara was fidgeting around and pulling at her jean shorts. Even though it was the tenth of October, the temperature didn't reflect it and the forecast predicted a high of seventy-eight degrees, allowing them the luxury of summer attire.

"That's what you get for drinking a forty-four-ounce Pepsi on the car ride," Sharanda sounded. "I don't feel one bit sorry for you."

"Thirty dollars?" Greg surveyed the painted wooden sign that displayed the price at the entrance. He lifted some money from his wallet, counting through the fanned-out cash.

Josh looked at his best friend, asking, "What about it?"

"It was twenty-five bucks last year!" Greg tucked the wallet away and promptly lit a cigarette. "What could they have possibly improved in twelve short months to warrant a five-dollar price hike?"

"They hired me," a soft voice came from behind. The four friends, one by one, turned to see a woman dressed in what looked like a purple Druid robe with a hood. She wore several gold bracelets and silver rings on her greyish fingers. A particular ring on her left hand resembled an eye with a crimson pupil. "I'll see you inside," she continued, brushing past them before anyone could respond, disappearing through the employee entrance.

***

Cara hadn't had much luck locating a prospective scapegoat. The Faire had been active since Labor Day and with only a few weeks to go, her time was running thin. She fiddled with the eye-ring on her index finger as her thoughts raced, approaching the tent that she would call home for the remainder of the weekend. The sign next to the cloth opening read:

Cara, the Hypnotist. First session, $5.00.

Beneath all the makeup and hooded robe, her flesh was decomposing, peeling, sloughing off more with each passing day. The robe had become a necessary inconvenience to conceal her rare affliction, even on uncomfortably humid days. She looked forward to a time when she could shed its weight and display her normally porcelain complexion with confidence.

White shock hit when she entered the tent. It was a familiar face, but one she hadn't seen in quite some time. The man was thin, young; handsome and he appeared... concerned. He recoiled at her shocking appearance while his serrated eyes slid over her. "You're in free-fall," he said flatly. "Pull the ripcord."

Cara looked around and unhitched her shoulder bag, putting it down on the main table in front of her. She lowered her hood and asked, "What are you doing here? I haven't seen you in almost—"

"—One year. Yes, but you've given me no choice."

"I really don't care what you have to say," she snapped back. "Now, I'd appreciate it if you left." The sight of the man, Timothy, had drained her energy even further than it had been and she found herself having to slide into the uncomfortable foldout chair to rest. Although handsomely rugged, his image churned her stomach. This was the man responsible for her current condition, the man responsible for her almost-certain death sentence, as displayed on her finger in the form of a crimson ring, bonded to its grip until her duty was fulfilled.

"I've noticed you haven't found a candidate yet," he chastised her. "I have almost as much of a vested interest in your success as you do. Don't forget that."

"Rest assured, it won't be long now," she countered. "I can feel it."

***

Greg's legs were asleep sitting on the uncomfortable wooden bench at the front of the small outdoor amphitheater. He was watching the Sultry Sirens of Sin, one of many shows they'd caught that day. Several of the experiences had

134

been dull, including a terminally lame magician who'd dropped his trick deck, spilling it across the stage, inducing a discord of boos.

This show was different. It was one reason he continued to attend the Ren Faire each year and he looked forward to the ladies' bawdy antics. His favorite part of the performance had always been when they selected an unsuspecting gentleman from the crowd to bridge the gap between performer and spectator. They would invite him on center stage, seating him in a chair where they proceeded to make a complete fool of the sucker in question, dancing around him, force-feeding him questionable fare and squeezing their breasts together inches from his face. Each man perpetually wore a look of astonished embarrassment, a fake-serious expression while their eyes ping-ponged across the amused audience.

And Josh, currently tethered to the Sirens' wooden seat of despair, was no exception. Greg glanced to his left and watched Barb spill the overpriced mead from her cheap plastic glass due to laughter, recording Josh's whole on-stage experience with her iPhone.

When you've been engaged as long as Josh and Barb and together even longer, jiggling boobs in front of your uncomfortable fiancée is nothing but YouTube gold.

"Should we put him out of his misery?" one of the Sirens called to the audience. A cacophony of responses sounded from the crowd, mixing opinions together. But ultimately, the Sultry Sirens of Sin released Josh from captivity, allowing him to leave the stage and join Barb on the bench. He grinned, appearing to be relieved.

The Sirens concluded their performance, bidding everyone farewell as Barb showed him the captured video on her phone. "You're not posting that on YouTube," he said. It wasn't a question, not much of a statement, either. It was a demand.

"We'll see," was Barb's response.

Outside on the main pathway, Sharanda examined the Renaissance Faire's map, scanning the show schedule as they ambled toward the Living Chess Board and merchant area. "You guys want to check out the 'Archery through the Ages' exhibit?" She kept going without waiting for a response. "Or what about the glassblowing demonstration?"

Greg lit a Marlboro and fanned the smoke away from Sharanda while she fake-coughed. He knew she hated smoking and didn't want to be rude.

While leaning on Josh's shoulder to steady her balance, Barb tagged down the rest of her mead and wiped away the remaining condensation from her lips. She held up her plastic glass, the one with O'MALLEY'S POURHOUSE written across the side, belched and said, "Sharanda," a bit exaggerated, "does it look like I want to go to some fucking glassblowing demonstration?"

"How about you slow down?" Josh suggested, swiping the glass from her grip. "You've already had five and it's not even noon."

Barb's eyes ticked over the intersection where they stood, visoring her flushed face from the sun's intrusion. "Isn't this Swashbuckler's Grove?" she managed, glancing around, puzzling out the geography through hazy alcohol-induced vision. "Look, right there." She pointed to a grove across the way. "The Anchor and Mermaid Tavern, I can get a refill there." She looked at Josh. "And if you try to stop me, that video will be on my YouTube channel faster than our last sexual encounter."

Greg watched Barb haul-ass to the Mermaid Tavern, Josh in tow. "Are we supposed to wait here?" Greg stage-whispered to Sharanda.

"I don't know what we're supposed to do." She rolled up the map and slid it into the back pocket of her cut-offs. "But I need a breather from her bullshit. Let's walk around a while. They can text us when they're ready to meet up."

Greg agreed and lit another cigarette.

***

It was noon in Ren town and Cara had only entertained one customer. The festival crowd had all but ignored her inviting five-dollar first session offer.

Maybe I can hypnotize these assholes into forking over their money, she wondered. But it

137

didn't work like that, unfortunately. They had to agree.

"You need to be more persuasive, Cara," Timothy suggested. "Remember how I was with you?"

"That wasn't persuasion on your part," she countered. "It was gullibility on mine. I didn't take you seriously." She wanted to rebuke him, but one thing was apparent: he'd fully duped her one year ago. She glanced down at the ring that he once possessed, now poisoning her own mortality.

It seemed not long ago that she'd encountered the man, Timothy, a hypnotist, at a strip mall in Staten Island, New York. He was charming to a fault, seemingly unreal. He wore a long silver robe, similar in style to the one that now imprisoned her. She didn't realize it, but its appearance was not for show. It was to hide his chilling skin condition. Cara had no interest in hypnotism, mostly because she thought it was bullshit, but she figured it might be interesting to try something new on that particular day.

Timothy had posed one simple suggestion at the time, but it would alter her life in ways she couldn't imagine. "How would you like to be a killer?" It caused Cara to bristle. She was thinking more along the lines of something fun, like a Disney Princess. But since she didn't really believe in this nonsense, she laughed and said, "Sure, whatever you say. But let's make it quick because I have to pick my husband up at noon."

138

The hypnotist did as she asked and within five minutes, she was on her way. Cara's husband, Victor, had been the first to die. It happened so quickly he didn't see it coming, the butcher knife sheathing into the side of his neck as he entered Cara's Subaru. She experienced no remorse, no emotion.

She swiftly moved on to her next victim, a middle-aged woman alone in her living room. Cara used the same knife and even rinsed the blood off in the dead woman's sink. She periodically checked her watch because Timothy had mentioned something during the hypnosis session:

"You have until nightfall to fulfil your duty, no less than five victims." She didn't know what that meant initially, but he clarified as she was leaving. "Cara," he said, prompting her to turn and face him. "Listen to me carefully. The hypnosis will lift once the sun sets. If you haven't reached a murder count of five, you won't live to see the morning and neither will I." She did fulfil her count that day and Timothy's curse had successfully transferred to her. He was free, but only momentarily.

"You need to sit in front of the tent, Cara," Timothy demanded, snapping her from the retrospective daydream. "People will see you out there. Only one customer today is pathetic. Do I have to remind you that in less than—"

"No, you don't!" Cara was more than aware of her situation. She had less than three weeks to find a replacement, or her time would expire and so

139

would she, decomposing into a pool of sludge, just as Timothy repeatedly warned. But Cara would also need to be selective. If the person she chose failed to carry out the task, well, she wouldn't have to wait weeks because their fate would be hers at sundown. Cara considered herself a good judge of character and repeatedly told herself not to settle for the first one. She'd have to be absolutely sure that this person was capable. So the elderly and handicapped were automatically disqualified in her eyes. It was nothing personal.

Cara's energy levels had worsened in the last month, but they had declined even further over the previous few days. She almost didn't care. Maybe it would be a blessing to die, let him deal with this shit, she often told herself. At least I'll be free.

"Our main goal now is to keep the ring moving forward," Timothy continued, "not reversing down the line." His vested interest rested in one elementary fact: if she failed to find a replacement, the cursed ring would transfer to him, infused to his flesh. Timothy's cycle would then restart all over. He'd again have to locate a willing replacement within the year. If he failed, the ring would then jump to the person who initially hypnotized him and so on. He recalled how difficult it was to locate a willing recipient and he could see the trouble Cara was having. He didn't want to go through that ordeal again.

Timothy snapped his fingers. "Cara, I have an idea." He sat across from her, his enthusiasm high.

140

"Look at where we are. What if we presented the hypnosis as some sort of game, like a role-play? We could explain that they'd be the killer and the would-be victims are pre-planned willing participants, all make-believe. It might just work."

Cara laced her fingers together as the information sank in. "Yeah," she muttered. "Let's get started."

With Timothy's help, she hefted herself out of the foldout chair and dragged her accoutrements outside. Cara sat by the tent entrance while the afternoon sun pressed down on her shoulders, eyes fastened to a lanky pale man smoking a cigarette and a young woman in cut-off shorts studying a brochure.

***

Ding! Greg's text alert sounded, or so he thought. When he thumbed on his screen, it was a YouTube notification. Barb had posted Josh's degrading experience for the world to see. Sharanda's phone buzzed a moment later, receiving the same alert. She laughed after opening the thumbnail and said, "It looks like she went ahead and did it."

"I'm sure Josh will try and make her take it down," Greg said, returning the phone to his pocket and tossing the burned-down Marlboro to the gravel, crushing it under the heel of his grey and black Converse. "I honestly don't know why he even cares."

They briefly stood and watched the participants of the massive Living Chess Board hop from one square to another, attempting to checkmate the other team's king.

"I wonder how many more fallen soldiers Barb has accumulated," Greg spoke up as he watched a bishop topple a rook on the board.

"Well, hello," a small voice cut in from behind. They both craned around, noticing the familiar woman they encountered at the front gate. Her rings and bracelets flared sharply in the light. "I recognized both of you from earlier and figured I'd ask how you were enjoying the Faire so far?"

Sharanda shrugged. "It's good - so far."

Greg looked beyond the woman's weary gaze, over her shoulder and spotted a tall man wearing an old-style red and black evening suit with a splash-of-plaid. His arms were crossed tightly across his chest, apparently deconstructing their interaction with great interest. "Yeah, it's fine," Greg brayed after a moment, wondering at the same time why this woman had blatantly interrupted him. A harsh rip of static came from a surrounding speaker, reminding the guests to attend the joust later that afternoon.

"I just love the joust," the woman said. "It's one of my favorite aspects of the Faire." Greg winced at her hollow banter, attempting to decipher her motive. He salvaged his pack of Marlboros from his pocket and tapped a cigarette out. "Oh, you can't smoke here. There are designated areas for that."

"Since when?" Greg asked, returning the cigarette. It must've been some new rule because he'd never heard of it.

"I'm not sure. But my employers reinforced that point when I was hired, even though I don't smoke." The woman's eyes slid up from Greg's pack. "So, uh, I think I might be able to help you." She motioned to his cigarettes. "Just come with me."

Greg's phone sounded again as he and Sharanda followed the woman past the restrooms and up the hill. The tall man had already rushed inside when he saw their approach, as if to pretend he wasn't scrutinizing their exchange the entire time. When Greg examined his phone, a text popped up from Josh:

Where are u guys?

At some hypnotist's tent across from that big ass chessboard. Come meet us.

What the hell are you doing there?

She thinks she can help me quit smoking.

Yeah, good luck with that. See u in a few.

"I'm Cara, by the way," the woman said, motioning to some empty seats around the table. "Please, sit."

***

143

Josh watched the hot mess formerly known as Barb stagger along the pathway, leaving an accidental trail of curly fries and paper ketchup cups littered across Town Crier's intersection. Somehow though, she managed to isolate her mead from any sort of spillage. She displayed smeared Cheese Whiz on her chin but didn't seem to notice.

Josh was still furious that Barb had posted the video on her YouTube channel while he was in the bathroom. He'd only been gone five minutes, but that's all it took. He was too exhausted to deal with it now, electing to salvage the day instead—especially since his attempts to curb her escalating mead purchases had failed.

They shuffled down Privy Lane where Josh noticed a blue tent directly across from the Human Chess Board, just as Greg had explained. He gripped Barb under her arm and assisted her up the grassy hill. He thumbed his phone on and dialed Greg's number.

Voicemail.

He hung up as they entered the darkness of the tent, just in time to see Greg stand up from the table. Sharanda stood to the left, hands in pockets. The tall man seemingly had no interest in anyone but her. His eyes had not deflected and nor had hers. She continued a dead stare as if their paths might've once crossed, like they knew each other.

"What is this?" Barb managed. "Josh, where are we?"

Greg laughed and said, "Well, apparently I just got hypnotized into quitting smoking."

"No fucking way," Barb countered in her patented slurred tone.

"Yes fucking way," he said, continuing his mockery. "I'm cured."

Cara caught on to his ridicule. "Make fun all you want," she said. "You'll see." She stood and introduced herself to the couple standing at the entrance. "Only five dollars for the first session," she offered. "What do you say?"

***

Josh couldn't believe he agreed to it: A killer? What was he thinking? Still, much like Cara before him, he put no stock in this nonsense. He initially wanted no part of hypnosis, but she'd been so persuasive, explaining that it was just some sort of pre-planned game. He allowed the hot mess, Barb, first honors while he considered it. The whole process only took a few minutes. She sat in a chair across from Cara while Josh and Greg looked on. Timothy silently stood to the tent's far left, his face distorted in the fractured shadows, gaze still locked on Sharanda. He suppressed a smile as he watched her fidget uncomfortably.

"When you open your eyes," Cara explained, "you will have no desire to touch another drink." She snapped her fingers and Barb awoke from her daydream, eyes fuzzed, mind clouded. It had been

Josh's idea to place her on the wagon. Surprisingly, there were no protests from her, simply because she believed it was a novelty act. "I've never been hypnotized before," she stammered. "That was fun."

When it was Josh's turn, he sat down across from Cara and watched her strike a match, igniting a black candle while wisps of smoke rose up. She hadn't done that ritual with his other friends and he wondered what made him so special. "I need 'nother drink!" Barb sounded.

Josh quickly turned. "No! Don't you dare!"

"Calm down," she fired back, throwing the tent flap open, allowing the outside light to smack the interior. Josh was about to stand when Cara gripped his wrist.

"Let her go," she said. "It'll be fine."

Sharanda sighed and said, "I'll follow her. You can finish up here."

Thankful for Sharanda's attentiveness, Josh nodded and turned to Cara. "I thought she'd have no desire for another drink?"

Barb had been out of the chair no longer than thirty seconds before initiating a mead excursion. If Josh had any doubts about Cara's abilities before, the bullshit level had just throttled to the exosphere.

"She doesn't have the desire," Cara reassured him. "She just isn't aware yet. May we begin, please?"

Josh nodded and rested his elbows on the table. "So I was thinking, Barb makes me watch these

146

awful reality shows. It's pure torment. Maybe you can hypnotize me into liking them, or at least making them tolerable?"

Timothy approached and handed Cara a folded envelope, along with a pen and another black candle. She struck a match and held it up, watching it hypnotically burn down. "I have something else in mind for you," she explained with a Cheshire grin. "I need you to sign this contract before we get started." Timothy unfolded the document and placed it before Josh. With eyes still fastened to the flame, Cara crossed the match to the wick immediately before it would've seared her flesh, and said, "It's just standard procedure."

"Standard procedure for what?" Greg spoke up. "I never signed anything." He lumbered over and lifted the document. Cara appeared distressed, her breath choked out as she attempted a response. Luckily, she didn't have to because a guttural display of laughter came from Greg as he tossed the document onto the table.

"What a crock of shit," he said, continuing his laughing fit. "A serial killer, right. Go ahead, buddy, knock yourself out," Greg added, clapping his hand on Josh's shoulder. "I need to go outside and make a phone call."

Timothy handed Josh the document after Greg walked out. "As I said, it's just a formality," Cara reiterated.

Josh held up the pen and studied its sharp, wicked point.

***

Greg Russo watched the faux wenches and knights pass by as he plopped down on the grassy hill and examined the four missed calls on his phone's screen. Why his boss, Kimberly, was bothering him on a Saturday was beyond him. He regretted not putting the ringer on silent to avoid precisely this kind of nonsense.

Of all his friends, he was the one who'd advanced the least in his chosen field. He majored in art history, which meant, unbeknownst to him at the time that he'd probably be working minimum wage the rest of his life. He'd gone from mopping up puke at the Shake Shack to his current retail hell at a Sports Zone, also mopping up puke.

He checked his messages and noticed a succession of "urgent alerts" from Kimberly, a bubbly type-A personality that happened to be eleven years his junior.

Greg! Tina and Aiden BOTH called out this afternoon! I'm desperate, call me!

In addition to being younger, she was also an idiot because he'd mentioned his Renaissance Faire trip to her several times. It was stress he didn't need and he retrieved his pack of cigarettes out of habit.

Ding, another message:

This isn't good! It's holy fuck territory!! Call or text me, seriously!

He gently thumbed his lighter and started typing:

I'm sorry, Kim, but I can't help you. At the Ren Faire all day, remember? C U on Tuesday.

He spun the lighter striker wheel and touched the flame to his Marlboro, thinking about adding a winking emoji but decided against it. A moment after he hit send, he puffed deeply on his cigarette. The smoke wafted into his lungs and a putrid sensation occurred. It was on par with sucking in the remains of fully decomposed roadkill.

Greg instantly turned on his knees and gagged, like a punch in the gut, flicking the cylinder-shaped culprit onto Privy Lane's adjacent walkway. His text alert dinged again, but he barely heard it over the sound of funnel cake and stale pizza regurgitating onto the grassy hill. He was purging so hard that he began to catch the attention of passing onlookers.

When the nausea subsided after approximately five minutes on his knees, Greg turned and sat, exhausted, and attempted to process his recent trauma. The roadkill taste remained on his tongue, spiking up to his nostrils and causing stomach flips.

"Oh God," he managed while choking back the rancid sensation. He held his abdomen as he clambered to his feet. The event had occurred so quickly and intensely that it left him shell-shocked. He ripped the Marlboro pack from his front pocket and studied the vile printing. With one swift squeeze, he crushed the remaining cigarettes into a pile of leafy powder and tossed them to the ground. He decided right there to never have another cigarette for as long as—

Greg winced as a dark thought washed over him and slowly turned towards the hypnotist's tent. Everything seemed to go quiet, except for a harsh breeze whipping the tent nylon and the atonal sounds of isolated flute music somewhere in the distance.

He recalled the document presented to Josh. How he believed it was nonsense, the same way he thought he couldn't be cured of his nicotine addiction. It wasn't possible, but somehow Cara possessed actual abilities.

Maybe the process hadn't yet been complete. I need to stop her, he thought while darting towards the tent's entrance, the worn-down soles of his Converse All-Star's slipping across the lawn in an anxious effort.

Greg pushed the tent flap aside and was met with a row of five meticulously placed black candles carefully spaced inches apart on the table. The flames pulsed with a thrum of energy. It wasn't entirely clear, but according to what Cara's document stated, he assumed each represented a human life not yet snuffed out.

The tent was strangely vacant. Empty foldout chairs scattered the interior and Josh and Cara and the tall man had disappeared.

The candle on the far right began to vibrate and shake on its own, as if someone was rapidly moving it side-to-side. The impossible sight forged denial in Greg, grinding against his nerves. He fell back a step, distancing himself as the far-right candle abruptly ceased vibrating and the flame died.

Greg Russo stumbled outside into the harsh light and realized death had arrived.

***

Josh hadn't wanted to use the knife. It felt uncomfortable in his hand, even with his newly-minted murderous urges. In addition, the young woman appeared as if she'd been having so much fun wading around in the Mud Pit attraction that he almost second-guessed the whole thing. However, it was only a fleeting moment before the impulses screamed back to life.

The contract he'd signed mentioned his own demise if he hadn't fulfilled a murder count of five before sundown, but the print was so small he hadn't initially noticed it. Before he signed, Cara had explained that this was nothing more than a fun novelty experience, where the victims were willing participants in a game. He understood now that this was no game. His personality had been seriously altered. No one was "in on it," so to speak. These were genuine victims.

Josh took advantage of his window of opportunity when the woman slipped behind the pit to use the rinsing station. The location was to the far north edge of the Faire, with nothing but bushes and a high castle wall that divided the outside area. It was intended to add atmosphere but also acted as a barrier to keep undesirables out. Undesirables meant anyone not willing to pay the admission fee.

His legs moved before he willed them, but he accepted it with a surge of excitement. The butter knife he'd recently obtained at the Nachos of Nottingham bounced around loosely in his front pocket, but it was only on reserve for emergencies. He noted the mini-dumpster located against the back wall as he rounded the corner, secretly hoping it wasn't full.

The woman was alone, caked in mud… and very, very clothing challenged. She wore an electric-pink bikini which Josh hadn't noticed due to the layered suit of mud armor previously plastered to her body. She stood under the gushing water which struck her tanned flesh in a succession of laser-thin streams while a cascade of brown, watery goo filtered down the small of her back. She seemingly hadn't noticed Josh watching because she continued as if auditioning for a Sports Illustrated Swimsuit issue.

A cascade of muddy fluid hugged the sides of Josh's Nike sneakers with each calculated step while he advanced on the unsuspecting woman. She slipped a crop of platinum blonde hair through her fingers and rinsed the long strands under the running water, still oblivious to the presence behind her.

And it would've remained that way if she hadn't turned.

"Excuse me," she said, moving aside when she noticed his continuing approach. A pulse in the woman's neck fluttered when Josh lunged at her throat with both hands, prompting her to attempt a scream. His thumb pressed on her windpipe, choking out her breath and all that expelled was a small squeak. The stream of water pressed down on them as the woman scratched and clawed at Josh's arms and he thought he heard her say, "Why are you doing this?"

It was probably his imagination, but he responded in turn. "Because you're convenient." Josh couldn't believe the fight she had, even biting his hand, puncturing his skin and drawing rivulets of blood. But he didn't flinch through the adrenaline rush.

It was taking too long, though.

Josh released her throat and gripped her forehead. Shifting his body weight forward, he repeatedly thrust the back of her head against the cement wall. The first slam fractured her skull, caving it inward and puncturing the cerebellum. The second slam had been followed by a gurgle, painting the wall red, causing the woman to fall limp in his arms. But Josh didn't let up. He continued his barbaric ritual, over and over, slamming her head no less than eleven times until his hands were scarlet soaked. Luckily, there'd been a jetting stream of water directly next to him, which he took advantage of.

He propped the woman's body against the wall. Her head slumped down and her lifeless eyes remained open, fixating on him. "Don't fucking look at me." He proceeded to hold a conversation with her as if she could hear him. "It's nothing personal," he insisted as he rinsed the gore from his palms. "I really had no choice."

"Brittany!" A voice came from his right. When Josh craned his neck, he saw a young man, also covered in mud and holding a hand over his mouth from shock.

The last thing he needed was mud man running off to get help, halting his progress on only the first victim. He thought quickly. "I think this woman slipped and hit her head," he said. "I need your help!"

The man frowned and blank shock slid across his eyes. He repeated the name, Brittany. "She's, she's my sister. I need to call an ambulance!"

"Wait," Josh insisted with soft intensity. "Come over here and help me elevate her head."

Mud man hesitated, apparently puzzling out the circumstances. After a brief moment, he darted to her sister's side. "I don't think she's breathing," he managed. "Call a goddamned ambulance!"

Josh hefted himself up and stood behind the emotionally fractured man, pretending to thumb his phone on. With an innocent curiosity, he watched the frantic man lightly tap his sister's cheeks, attempting to jar her awake. "Brits," the man repeated. "Please, say something."

The second hand on Josh's watch seemed to tick louder, reminding him of his time constraint. "They're on their way," he said, putting his phone in his pocket and at the same time palming the stainless steel handle of the butter knife.

The man turned and, through suspicion, said, "But I, I didn't hear you speaking to anyone."

Josh stepped towards him and white-knuckled the handle, leering down into the dead woman's glazed eyes. "That's because I didn't call." Josh allowed mud man to view the dull blade for a moment. The instant he attempted to stand, Josh sprung the blade forward, catching the left side of the man's cheek, yet missing any vital organs.

Josh momentarily cursed himself for missing his mark before making another attempt. The man's shock turned to anger and he caught Josh's wrist before any further damage was inflicted.

"What is this shit?" mud man said while twisting Josh's wrist, causing a sharp sinister pain to shoot up to his elbow. One arm was incapacitated, so he balled a fist with the other and drew back. He landed a solid blow on the man's nose with a dull pop, rupturing the cartilage and inducing a spatter of scarlet.

Mud man stumbled and caught his foot on his sister's right leg, throwing him off balance. The wall halted his fall, allowing him to regain his footing. He appeared disoriented and gripped his nose while blood laced between his fingers.

The sound of the man blabbering some incoherent gibberish and a stream of running water ran through Josh's ears, causing a high-pitched ringing.

He decided to finish what he started. Josh Capra, the kind of guy who would typically give anyone the shirt off his back, advanced on the weakened man. He raised the knife to eye level and sheathed the four-inch blade into the man's trachea. His face twisted into denial as he fell back onto his sister, gasping for air as a runnel of warm blood ticked rhythmically from his neck-wound.

Josh hadn't planned on using the knife. Still, the first kill had proven too complicated, and he had no intention of bashing another head against the wall—especially with the perpetual risk of a third person coming round the corner. He frantically rinsed the blood-stained blade and analyzed the siblings' serene display, their heads resting on each other's shoulder.

A sharp voice cut in from behind, snapping him back. "You have to hide the bodies." Josh spun and caught a glimpse of the hypnotist and her sidekick. "If you don't properly conceal them, the entire plan will unravel," Cara explained.

Josh nodded and looked back at the siblings. "How did you find me?"

"It's not a very big place. We've been keeping an eye on your progress. Not bad, but you still have three victims left and we're here to make sure you stay on schedule."

Timothy hung around the entry point and kept watch for random intruders. "Cara," he said with a firm tone, intended to keep her on schedule.

"Right." She glanced at the mini yellow and black waste disposal unit to her left. "This dumpster will hold no more than two bodies, so you need to go elsewhere. Just leave the cleanup to us. Now, get moving."

***

Barbara Connelly's regurgitation, Curly Fries and Cheese Whiz, swam in a coagulated mess on the muddy grounds of a designated smoking area. This occurred immediately after acquiring an additional honey mead, her first since the hypnosis session and eighth overall for the day. Sharanda had attempted to curtail her consumption but was met with the same contempt that Barbara had dropped on Josh.

"I think you're done for the day," was evidently not the words Barb wanted to hear and countered with a volley of sarcastic, hurtful responses. With mead in hand and Sharanda in tow, they'd entered the smoking section where Barb bummed a cigarette from an unsuspecting teenage girl wearing a Xena outfit. She had even resembled Lucy Lawless in stature and facial structure.

Shortly after dragging on the Newport, Barb sampled the mead. That's when the mistake occurred. Her face balled up from the vile liquid and she dropped to her knees, purse spilling open, expelling an assortment of lipstick shades and eyeliner.

Sharanda darted to Barb but was unable to pull her up. "What the fuck," she spouted between sheets of barf. "It tastes like toxic waste." Xena looked on, seemingly unfazed, puffing out smoke rings while her attention zigzagged from her replica Claymore sword to Barb's guttural display.

Sharanda's phone dinged another text alert. It was the fifth message from Greg, who'd been attempting to locate them for the last twenty minutes. They were never settled in one location for too long, due to Barb's constant wandering.

True to her reputation, once the final purge had ceased, she was on her feet sauntering out of the smoking area. Sharanda was tired of her insatiable behavior and fired another text to Greg.

Forget that last message. Barb took off again, so don't meet us at the smoking area. I'll keep you posted. And to answer your previous question, no, I haven't seen or heard from Josh.

Sharanda thumbed her phone off and glanced up in time to notice Barb disappear into a crush of inebriated fairgoers. "Christ," she hissed and hurried through the crowd, trailing closely behind. "Barb! Wait up!" she called after her.

Timothy wheeled the mini dumpster containing the dead bodies back to the tent. They were more burdensome than expected and it didn't help that he had to haul them from the Mud Pit, past the Feasting Glen and the Castle Gates. Then they went left across Beggar's Crossing and the Picnic Grove, eliciting several stares every time one of the dead siblings' limp extremities slammed against the interior.

The inside of his suit was soaked with perspiration and he sensed relief when the tent appeared ahead. "Cara," he said plainly. "I should mention that the one before me is here, a woman. I noticed her earlier today."

Cara slowed and dabbed streaky makeup with a tissue. "Here? Are you sure?"

"Oh yes, I'm certain of it," he said as they entered the tent. The shade felt good and he immediately dropped the waste unit next to the table. Timothy noted the two extinguished candles. A third subtly vibrated.

***

Josh Capra would've ordinarily felt crushing remorse for the teenage girl whose face was grounded in puke, impaled by a sword of his own doing. Still, he admired her Xena: Warrior Princess cosplay attire.

He'd been trailing Barb and Sharanda for around ten minutes, ever since the Ball and Chain Tavern where Barb spent more of his money on alcohol. He kept his distance while they traveled north on Bacchus Boulevard towards the New World Fountain square and the smoking area's general vicinity. It was their last known location because a frivolous distraction by a Faire actor on high stilts had side-lined his pursuit. It was his damn fault. His ADD had taken over and he stopped to watch the man wander around the square, fiercely juggling a collage of multi-colored batons while onlookers snapped photos.

That's when everything plunged south. Stilt man clopped on by and Josh lost track of his prey. It happened that fast. In a fit of panic, he last-minute checked the smoking area and noticed Xena in battle-stance with a cigarette one hand, conducting light saber exhibitions while she spun a replica Claymore sword with the other.

Replica or not, the thing was made of a sort of metal and possessed a sharp sinister blade, capable of inflicting harm. It reminded Josh of the naysayers who criticized '80s wrestling as bullshit. Sure, it was fake, but performers could and did get hurt. It was the same situation with this lady's would-be prop.

Josh laced his fingers together and cleared his throat, catching Xena's attention. "Love your costume. May I?" he said, motioning to the Claymore.

***

The last message Greg received from Sharanda was to meet at the smoking area. That was right before his phone went dead. The battery had been on a downward trend for the last six months, functioning for only half a day before needing a charge. Without the capability to replace it on his Galaxy S7 and the inability to afford a new phone, he'd been perpetually stuck with the useless piece of junk until his funds told him otherwise. He was typing a message when his phone powered down:

Listen, stay away from Josh. Whatever U do, just don't

And that was it. The screen went dark.

He cursed the rectangular paperweight as he forged towards their designated meeting place, pushing forward through the herd of fairgoers in seemingly lockstep formation as they moved towards the Ultimate Horse Joust.

A rumbling in Greg's stomach side-lined him briefly, so he stopped for a pretzel and a beer. Designated driving be damned. He devoured it swiftly and instinctively reached in his pocket for a Marlboro before recalling the traumatic incident on the hill, which induced a shudder.

The once crowded square was beginning to thin by the time Greg arrived. The smoking area was just ahead. He downed the rest of the brew and tossed out the plastic cup before entering the secluded oasis of the smoking section.

If he'd still been grasping his food and beverage, they would've slipped from his grip, and fallen in a free-fall of dismay. What Greg witnessed was not Barb or Sharanda, as he expected, but something entirely different. He fell back a step at the vision of Josh standing over a very young woman in a cosplay outfit. She was on her knees hunched over, her face resting in a pool of scarlet liquid, mixing with the aftermath of Barb's regurgitation. A long sword had been embedded in the back of her skull, skewering out through her left eye socket, the front blade running into the moist soil, piecing the puke and cascading blood. Josh's hand remained on the hilt and he proceeded to twist the blade sideways.

"Jesus Christ," Greg cried and Josh swiftly darted his eyes away from his victim, looking at Greg.

"My friend," Josh began. "I'm surprised to see you. Please, come here."

Greg was aware that this person was not Josh, having no control of his actions. "You have to stop this," Greg rushed to add, attempting to curb Josh's intentions.

Josh tightened his grip around the handle and extracted the blade from the woman's skull. Pieces of brain and a segment of her eyeball dripped from the wicked point, sheeting down and finger-painting the back of her bare arms and legs.

162

"And why would I want to do that?" Josh asked rhetorically. "I still have two more victims on my list."

Greg stepped backward when Josh moved away from Xena, slowly starting toward him while gently wiping off the blood-flecked blade with the fabric of his black Greta Van Fleet tee shirt.

"Where do you expect to go?" Josh asked; his voice sterner than before. Greg didn't understand the question. He was distanced enough from his pursuer to easily exit the smoking oasis.

"Fuck you, Josh," he continued backward. He was set to turn and enter the square's streets when he abruptly walked back into something. His progress halted.

A whisper in his ear followed. "Any luck with your smoking cessation?" A sharp kick to the back of his knee-joint came, dropping Greg on all fours. A gale of laughter sounded from Josh. And when Greg craned his neck upward, the unsettling image of Cara and Timothy peered down at his defeat.

The sun still burned in the sky, but everything appeared darker to Greg, eerier, like a lens filter had been placed over his vision. Another kick came, this time to his left ribcage—then a kick to his jawbone and one to his spine. Many more followed in rapid succession. Timothy and Josh alternated while Cara watched. The last thing Greg heard was Cara sounding off.

"Finish the job," she instructed, immediately before a Claymore blade impaled his gut.

***

Josh ditched the Claymore and allowed Cara and Timothy to dispose of it, along with Greg and Xena. Before he'd left the oasis, his friend's body had been dragged into a large sprout of hedges along the border of the smoking area. Josh wished he could've stuck around longer, but the sky was darkening, evening shade approaching. He had just one victim left and he continually repeated the words in his head. One more left.

It had been no less than ten minutes since he'd lost sight of Barbara and Sharanda, so he headed south on Beggar's Crossing towards the Bacchus free wine tasting pavilion, hoping to spot them along the way.

The crowded streets had become somewhat desolate, making it easier to find his target. Above the distant roars of the crowd at the Ultimate Joust were the familiar sounds of slurred speech within ear-shot. It became louder as Josh followed its source.

"I need to sit down!" Barbara demon hissed to Sharanda.

A ray of hope fell over Josh. Sure, there were plenty of other potential victims around, but he wanted to kill Barbara. She'd posted his humiliating experience on YouTube, even after he requested otherwise and he'd been fuming about it even before his hypnosis. It was payback time, though he needed to act quickly.

Sunset was at six-thirty. However, a quick time-check notched-down his confidence.

Six o'clock? How did that happen?

He thumbed off his phone in time to catch Barbara leading Sharanda into the Bacchus wine tasting grove. He entered the open pavilion, moved into their space and watched the duo claim their stools. It was just his luck; there were too goddamn many jesters and wenches invading the area. The whole fucking Faire was attending the joust, except for these assholes cadging a free buzz.

"I don't want anything," Barb said, swatting away the wine sample. Sharanda promptly tagged down both samples of Knight's Reward.

Time check: six-ten.

Josh Capra had twenty minutes to live unless he made a move. His breath was ragged; he gripped the butter knife handle and pulled it from his front pocket, continuing to hide it.

The ladies were no more than six feet away when they stood and wended around the left side of the bar. Josh hid behind a couple of wenches before emerging to pursue. He was looking to end it right there in front of a crowd when the ladies went out into the street. A pinch of relief stung him when they departed. It would've been messy, far from ideal and he would've been caught. This was the better option and he was grateful for it.

***

Barbara had wanted to visit the Fair's torture museum all day, but it was typically too congested during peak hours. With most of the horde at the joust, it was an opportune time.

"Let's go to that medieval dungeon place," she said while they walked in that direction. "You know; the one with all the torture devices."

"Yeah, fine," Sharanda answered, only half-listening. She was too preoccupied with thoughts of Greg and Josh and especially Timothy. The way he looked at her earlier in the tent, she was confident he'd recognized her. It was one of the reasons she'd gone after Barbara so quickly. It was the perfect excuse to leave.

There was also the issue of her two friends' radio silence. Greg hadn't responded to her messages lately and Josh had been completely MIA. She felt uncomfortable at the Faire and wanted to make tracks sooner than later, especially with Timothy skulking around.

The simple fact that Barb had been hypnotized into despising alcohol told her one thing: that Timothy's underling possessed legitimate abilities and, furthermore, had been actively seeking a replacement candidate.

Barbara tapped away on her phone and pressed send:

Not cool ignoring all my messages Josh! Where are U?

"Still hasn't responded?" Sharanda asked.

"The hell with him."

"Do me a favor and text Greg. Tell him to meet us at the Torture Museum."

***

Josh followed the two women into the museum entrance, concealing himself behind the doorway as Barb and Sharanda stopped to admire the iron maidens and breast ripper, cleverly placed in the admission area. It appeared as if the museum had been shuttered for the day due to the absence of a ticket-taker. The building was sectioned into pathways, exhibiting the most notorious forms of torture. Josh wondered if these devices were mere replicas or authentic pieces of the era, possibly used centuries ago. No other patrons wandered the halls.

They delved deeper into the exhibit. Josh couldn't see a reason to conceal his presence any longer. The place was barren.

A quick time check revealed six-twenty. He had ten minutes left, unless...

"So happy to see you all in one place," a deep voice came from behind, prompting the ladies to turn and catch Josh standing a short distance away. Josh wasn't the one who spoke. He wasn't alone. A strange expression crept across Sharanda's face when she realised Timothy was there, accompanied by Cara, her crimson ring glinting in the sharp light.

"Sharanda," Timothy was quick to speak. "It's nice to see you again. I've wanted to catch up for a long time." He paused and checked his silver wristwatch. "But that will have to wait. This young man has a job to do."

Barbara turned to Sharanda and asked, "Uh, what does he mean by that?"

"It means brace yourself."

***

Greg Russo had lost a lot of blood, not only from the Claymore gut wound but also from the succession of scrapes and cuts inflicted from lying in a thorn bush with Xena. Luckily, her costume contained numerous cloth garments that could double as a bandage. From his secluded sanctuary, he'd overheard Cara's mention of the torture museum. So when his prosecutors left the area, he crept out on hands and knees, removing thorns as he made his way to the clearing. Why would they leave a perfectly capable sword behind? He couldn't fathom their stupidity.

With a recently secured bandage cinched around his waist and newly acquired Claymore sword, Greg Russo lumbered slowly from the smoking area with only one thought:

Before you leave someone for dead, make sure they actually are. Morons.

***

Josh hadn't thought his plan through and made the idiotic mistake of listening to Timothy. "You have five minutes before sundown. Just pull your knife and stab the bitch!" he'd ordered, shouldering him forward. It had seemed pretty straightforward, so Josh complied and brought out the blade. What he hadn't counted on was the wooden display rack by the side of the ladies. It contained an assortment of weaponry which they'd utilized.

Sharanda stood in front of him and spun a weighted spiked mace, then advanced on Josh while Barbara stood in a battle stance, gripping the hilt of a sharp forty-one-inch Rapier blade.

"Why the hell did you make me leave that sword back at the smoking area?" Josh shot at Timothy, still backing away from the women and glancing at his pitiful butter knife.

"It was covered in that man's blood, you idiot. It would've brought too much attention."

"Would you do something, Josh?" Cara cut in, grasping a ripple of tee-shirt to jog his attention.

"Listen to me, Josh," Sharanda joined in. "Have you ever considered the prospect of those two people standing directly behind you, completely unarmed? They bleed, too."

Timothy fired a withering stare at Sharanda. "Are you crazy?" he stage-whispered. "Did you entirely forget about the rules? The ones you explained to me yourself?"

"Fuck the rules."

Barbara eyeballed Sharanda and asked, "What's he talking about?"

"It's not important," she said. Then moving back to Josh, she rushed to add, "If you come at me with that butter knife, I'll split your skull in two. Or you can turn around and take option B. I'm guessing you only have a few minutes to make a decision." Josh raised the knife, studying its metallic blade, and turned to face his companions, Sharanda's words echoing in his mind.

Timothy made calming hands. "Don't listen to what she's—"

The first stab caught Timothy just below his heart. A rose of scarlet bloomed through his evening suit and streaked down the outer lining after Josh pulled out the blade. He stumbled backward, clipping the glass window encasement of a guillotine exhibit. The second stab pierced the tendons of his raised hand, a defensive wound inflicted from a successful attempt at preventing the blade from entering his throat.

Cara stepped aside and didn't interfere. After all, she had nothing to lose with Timothy dead. He'd be the fifth victim, exempting both her and Josh from an excruciating demise. Josh's third attempt hit its mark, skewering Timothy's larynx, crunching his vocal cord and puncturing through to his vertebra, producing a bloody lava flow. He twisted the blade against the force of his victim's grasp until the pressure ceased and Timothy's arms dropped to his side, his body slithering down onto the floor, painting a single red brush-stroke against the glass.

Josh allowed the knife to remain in the man's neck, figuring he'd have no further use for it. Barbara crouched on the floor and shielded her eyes from Josh's impossible actions, her breathing ragged. Sharanda was a bit less traumatized. She remained upright and palmed the spiked Morning Star with both hands.

"So," Cara addressed her. "You're the one who preceded Timothy. I can imagine you're just as relieved as I am that this curse isn't heading backward in your direction."

Sharanda shook her head and lowered the weapon. "It only means that it continues on, marching toward a new destination. Josh will discover that soon enough."

Cara checked her watch. "We really cut it close that time. One minute to spare."

"I'm just relieved that my friends are okay," said Sharanda.

The sound of approaching footfalls cut through the silence. They intensified, coming closer. Someone, whoever it was, had entered the museum and was ambling in their direction. The audible silk of dragging metal against concrete sounded off the walls.

All ears perked up.

"What should we do?" Josh started, apparently seeking some sort of council. "If they find us here, we're—" Something halted his inquiry mid-sentence.

Greg appeared down the stretch of hallway and hobbled toward them. One hand pressed on his stomach, the other gripped the hilt of a familiar Claymore. He stopped when he reached Josh and Cara. He raised the blade and said, "Surprise, mother fuckers!" He managed a small grin and added, "You might want to recheck your math, Josh. Because according to my tally, you're one victim short."

Cara's alarm sounded, signing the official arrival of nightfall.

"Fuck me," was all Josh said.

It began with a guttural moan that escalated to heightened decibels. Cara's eyes popped at the sight of Josh's flesh dissolving, large chunks sloughing off, sliding away like dripping candle wax and mixing in a waterfall of sputum. It resembled Arnold Toht's face melting display in the finale of Raiders of the Lost Ark.

Then Cara joined him, mirroring Josh's horrific display. Her moans hit the rafters, blistering eardrums through echoes of her demise. In a brief moment of dismay, Cara, seemingly frightened to die alone, embraced Josh's sloughing abdomen. He returned the gesture and they continued their descent together.

It was clear that no one in the hallway expected to witness their friend Josh and the hypnotist dissolve into a puddle of liquid flesh. But that's exactly what'd happened, right before them. And they could never un-see Josh's jawbone separating from its joints, dangling for a moment before dropping off. Or Cara's eyeballs rolling out of her face to the ground, landing like a glop of mashed potatoes.

The duo met their fate in the form of a puddle. Once the act was complete, the sounds of Barbara's braying sobs could be heard down the hallways, through the rafters and out into the surrounding streets.

A blast of silence came, then a gentle hum that pulsed from Sharanda. She held up her hand, examining the crimson ring now cemented to her left index finger.

After a tight intake of breath, she said, "Shit! Not again!"

A Friend Of The Family
Diane Arrelle

Dennis drove slowly, squinting through the pollen-filled sun glare. He scowled as Ronny blithered on about summer in the Jersey Pine Barrens and his old girlfriend, Starlynne. Ron was the bore of the fraternity and Dennis really hated his endless droning stories.

In fact, he really hated Ron. That guy was a do-gooder, a 'study and get good grades' kind of creep. He wouldn't have even had to put up with Ron at all if his damned parents had paid the plane fare home. But no, they insisted he fend for himself, find a summer job, be a man. Thank God Ronny had invited him to their family cabin near the shore for the whole summer.

` Dennis gritted his teeth and swatted at the horse-flies competing with the mosquitoes for his blood. The dirt road under his tires churned out a cloud of dust and he felt a tickle deep in his throat. Finally they reached a rustic log cabin surrounded by an apparently unending forest of scrub pine trees.

He unfolded his long legs from the beat-up car he'd bought with the book and supply money his parents had sent him during the school year. He stretched and asked, "how far to the beach?"

Ronny sniffed the pine scented air like a puppy. "The river's about a mile to the west, the

174

back bay is about three miles southeast and the ocean's about fifteen miles due east. Atlantic City's about twenty miles from here. We're deep in the pines, real close to the home of Mother Leeds and her thirteenth child."

Dennis knew what was expected of him and decided to be polite. "Who?"

"Mother Leeds and her mystery child, kid number thirteen," Ronny answered, his voice deepening. "The Jersey Devil! The story goes that she had her last child on a stormy autumn night and as soon as he popped out, he spread bat wings and flew up the chimney."

"Really?" Dennis feigned interest.

"Yeah, really. That was a couple of hundred years ago, but he still lives around here. Starlynne says she's seen him lots of times."

"I'll have to meet this Starlynne, she seems like a fascinating girl."

"Oh, she is," Ronny gushed, leading the way to the cabin. "She is!"

He unlocked the heavy door. Dennis looked around at the glistening spider webs covering the wooden furniture and shuddered. What had he gotten himself into? "Parents don't get up here much, do they?"

"Actually they were here last week. The bugs and plants take over as soon as you turn your back. Only the real Pineys like Starlynne seem to have a rapport with them. She's a pine witch."

Dennis was getting tired of hearing about this stupid girl who was probably ugly to boot. An illiterate, red-necked hillbilly. A Piney. He'd never even heard the term till he crossed half the country to attend the University of Pennsylvania. Now, after spending two summers across the Delaware River at the Jersey Shore, he'd heard his fill of rural pine stories. There was the Jersey Devil to have to contend with, as well as mad murderers in the woods and sharks in the waters. Didn't these people have anything better to do than make up stories to scare the shit out of each other?

"So, Ronny," Dennis steered the conversation away from local lore. "What shall we do first, hit the beach or the casinos?"

Dennis loved the Jersey Shore. It was the land of opportunity. He knew that a good-looking guy like himself, tall and blond, was everything rich beach chicks looked for. He could be set for life if he got the chance. There had to be thousands of lonely women just waiting for the opportunity to help make his life perfect.

"Neither," Ronny said interrupting his thoughts. "I thought we'd just go for a hike, maybe see some deer and, if we're lucky, a couple of locals."

Dennis couldn't believe it; the stupid ass-wipe wanted to waste time on a nature walk. Better to go along with him for a while, he decided. After all, they had a whole month before Ronny's parents planned to use the cabin. Dennis figured if he

176

played his cards right, he'd get by all the summer vacation without having to get a job. He felt sure that he'd find some stupid broad to take him in for the other half of the summer, feeding him steak and caviar and buying him presents. Why, if he got real lucky, he could be out of this rural, bug-infested hell before the month was up.

He put on long jeans and sprayed himself with insect repellent. "Want some?" he offered Ronny the can as he eyed the guy's white arms and the pale, skinny legs sticking out of his shorts.

Starlynne taught me a little on how to get along with nature. The bugs and I have a sort of pact."

Dennis rolled his eyes. This guy was just too much. "Okay, it's your blood."

The hike was beyond boring. Just as Dennis expected, Ronny pointed out flora and fauna, as if anyone really cared about the stinking bunnies and squirrels. He talked on as Dennis swatted at mosquitoes that didn't seem to notice the maximum-strength repellent he was wearing.

Just as he was about to give up all hope that something interesting was going to happen, Ronny stopped short and yelled, "Hey, Starlynne! Over here!"

Dennis looked around and saw her. He sucked in air through clenched teeth, then whistled low. He stared at a vision walking across a field of weeds, only the weeds seemed to bloom in front of her as she approached. He knew that was silly and figured the breeze must be pushing the hidden wildflowers up. Yet the lavender and white flowers enhanced her glimmering beauty. She was white, pale like the snowy, bell-shaped buds that opened at her feet. Long golden-white hair hung past her shoulders.

He found himself crossing the field to meet her, although he didn't remember starting to walk. She smiled, color rushing to her cheeks as she walked right past him, holding out her hands to Ronny. Dennis stood, amazed. The guy who couldn't get a date if his life depended on it was hugging the most beautiful girl in the world.

Finally Ronny broke their spell. "Starlynne, I'd like you to meet Dennis."

Starlynne looked at Dennis and he noticed with fascination that her eyes, which at first appeared colorless, proved to be pale, early dawn blue. He grasped her partially extended hand and was surprised to feel her pull away. As he stared at her perfect features, all the color drained from her face, turning it chalk white. Her eyes widened and the pupils rolled up. She collapsed, folding slowly to the long grass.

"Holy shit!" Dennis said, stunned.

Ronny knelt down and cradled her head in his lap. "Star, Star," he whimpered, pushing back her hair as if she were a child in need of comforting.

Slowly the color returned to her waxy face and her eyes fluttered open. "Bad... so very, very bad," she whispered and started to cry.

178

"What's bad, Star? What's the matter?" Ronny asked, hugging her.

"N... n... nothing, it's all right," Starlynne said, getting up on shaky legs. "I'm fine now." She turned to Dennis and added, "I'm pleased to meet you." But she didn't extend her hand and she didn't smile.

Time seemed to stand still in the woods. By Saturday, Dennis was almost foaming at the mouth. He'd spent hours tearing the legs off spiders and the wings off dragonflies just to keep busy. He even welcomed an evening of miniature golf with Ronny and Starlynne at a tourist trap on Route 9. Starlynne, though she didn't actually ignore Dennis, seemed to avoid eye contact most of the evening. Occasionally he'd catch her sneaking a glance, but she'd quickly look away.

He finally got her full attention when they returned to his car. He dug through the trunk for one of the gifts he had picked up a few months back at an after Christmas sale. With a dramatic bow, he held out the gift-wrapped box to her.

Starlynne's cheeks flushed pink as she took the offered present. "For me?"

Dennis was constantly amazed by her sincere veneer. All girls expected gifts. He knew all about buying their lust. That's why he always kept a few gift-wrapped trinkets in the trunk, because, he knew that if he gave women enough trinkets, they all became whores and spread their legs.

179

He wanted Starlynne, at least for a few times. She really turned him on, just a glance from her made him hard. He wanted to feel her flesh next to his; he wanted to feel their sweat mingle. He wanted to taste her, relish her, have her. Then move on. After all, life wasn't rent-free and he'd need a babe to put him up by August and not in these stinking woods. The beach was calling him, but in the meantime, he'd buy Starlynne.

He watched her open the gift, smiled as her eyes grew round and she cooed at the cheap silver-plated candleholders. She smiled at him, the first real heart-felt smile he'd gotten from her since they met. "Oh, Dennis, they're lovely! Are they really for me?"

"Of course they are, Starlynne. Anybody who is such a good friend to my buddy Ron should have anything she wants."

"Oh thank you!" she said as she took Ronny's hand. Dennis stared at her like she'd slapped him. How could she take his gift then go to the jerk?

He smiled and shook his head. The bitch was playing hard to get...

The next day they went canoeing on the Wading River. The water was warm and shallow and smelled of summer. Dennis would have been bored on the tiny boat, except that Starlynne had his full attention.

He liked the way her breasts pushed up against the white fabric of her blouse as she helped Ronny paddle the watercraft. He wondered how she would feel beneath his fingers, his lips. He closed his eyes and could almost feel them making love. He could hear her moaning with pleasure and wanted to join in when he suddenly remembered that they were in a canoe.

He opened his eyes to see why she was moaning. Ronny had his arm tangled in a thorn branch. He was dripping ruby rivers over his fingers and hers as they grasped the wound.

"Dennis, help paddle! Please!" Starlynne pleaded.

Dennis pried the oar from Ron's bloody fingers. This ought to help improve my image with her, he thought as he used the oar and pushed off too hard. The small canoe tipped and everyone splashed into the murky water. He was surprised to discover the bottom thick with muck covering the remains of long dead trees and he wished he hadn't taken off his shoes.

With difficulty, he painfully waded to shore, trying not to catch his feet on the sharp stumps. He turned to see if Starlynne needed help. If he was lucky, maybe the idiot with her would drown. In fact, that was an excellent thought. If Ronny drowned, Starlynne would definitely turn to him, Ronny's best friend, for comfort.

Luck wasn't with him and the other two had also staggered to shore. Ronny was shaking, his teeth chattering and his head lolling back. He was barely conscious. Starlynne shooed Dennis away.

181

"I'll take care of this," she said and covered the gash with both hands and moaned deep in her throat. Dennis watched as the blood flowing between her white-knuckled fingers slowly stopped. He figured she was being a human tourniquet but when she removed her hands from the wound a few minutes later, the bleeding had completely ceased. She stood up, swaying, and staggered to the water's edge.

She dipped her skirt in the river, wiped the blood from her hands then went to Ronny and started washing him off.

"Hey, do you think that's a good idea, wetting that wound?" Dennis questioned. "He'll start bleeding again."

"No, he won't," she said.

When the arm was clean, Dennis stared in disbelief. The wound was gone. He could see a red line where the jagged cut had been, but even as he watched, it faded.

Ronny groaned, rolled over to his knees and threw up. "I'm sorry," he mumbled weakly. "I can't handle blood."

"Shhh," Starlynne said, "It's all right now."

Ronny smiled at her and Dennis was positive that if they had been alone they would both have left their virginity right there on the island.

Suddenly, Ron looked at Dennis and frowned. "Den, you're hurt, too! Starlynne, look, Dennis' foot is bleeding."

Dennis looked down and saw that he had sliced his foot. He sank to the ground as he suddenly became aware of the stinging pain.

Starlynne seemed to be having a non-vocal conversation with Ronny. Finally, she nodded.

Ronny smiled. "It will be okay," he said to her.

Starlynne got up and walked over to Dennis. She placed her hands on his foot and shuddered violently. He could feel her vibrating and wondered if being a healer hurt. As if in answer, she screamed and let go. "I'm sorry, I can't!" she sobbed. "I can't help you. Bad, so very, very bad!" She turned away and ran to the edge of the water.

"What does she mean by that?" Dennis demanded, angry that she'd used up all of her curative powers on Ronny.

"She's just drained, that's all," Ronny said standing up and offering a hand to Dennis.

"That's another thing," Dennis said, grasping Ronny's hand and pulling himself up. "She just about dies every time she has to touch me. You'd think the girl hated me or something."

"Nah," Ron said in a low voice. "She's just scared of you. She's a real innocent, not worldly like us. People scare her."

Dennis understood, she was scared all right. Scared of the feelings she felt when she was around a real man. Well, he just had to remember to go slow.

The guys righted the boat and the three of them paddled home in silence. Ron took Starlynne to her place and Dennis stayed at the cabin, cleaning his foot. The cut was superficial and had already stopped seeping.

When Ronny returned, he told Dennis about the tragedy surrounding Starlynne's family. "Her parents are dead," he explained in a hushed voice. "Bunch of rednecks got drunk on a windy, autumn night three years ago and went hunting for the Jersey Devil. Rumors always had it that her family housed the beast. Took it in whenever it got lonely. Anyway, the damn pineys burned them up. Set their house on fire with all of them sleeping inside. Starlynne was the only one to survive the fire. And you know what else, all those crazy murderous bastards, all of them disappeared."

Dennis snorted. "What do you mean, disappeared?"

"They all went out hunting or fishing at different times and none of them ever came back. The thirteenth Leeds child takes care of its friends."

"That's absurd!" Dennis said, laughing. "You don't really believe that crap?"

"As a matter of fact, I do. Starlynne told me how she escaped. It helped her, but she still scares easily. She swears she is going to die young. She's told me over and over again she's going to die a horrible, violent death and nobody, not even 'it', will be able to save her." Ron shuddered. "I hope she's wrong, I pray it, because I'm going to marry my bog witch. I plan to be with her forever."

"Well, enough of the pine lure for me," Dennis got up. "I'm going out to grab some sandwiches." He sat in his car and started to pull out onto the main dirt road, but turned into Starlynne's driveway instead. He walked up the steps, noting the wooden house was relatively new. He knocked and felt annoyed when she answered with a gasp. "You!"

"Yeah, me! Want to tell me why you hate me so?"

She hesitated.

"I'm alone," Dennis said, pushing past her. "Now look, I'm not some bad guy who'd hurt you or anything. So why do you pretend to dislike me?"

"You are bad," Starlynne whispered. "You are so bad that you are going to be my death. I felt it in your touch."

He laughed. "Bad? Hey look, baby, I'm just a regular guy. I've never hurt anyone, so you can be damned sure I'm not going to kill you."

She shook her head, "You are a bad person. Leave me and leave Ronny. He can't see you for what you are."

He stepped closer and grabbed her arms. "Look, Starlynne, let's drop all this witch crap. I don't know how you healed Ronny but I have a pain I'd like you to heal for me."

Still gripping her arms, he forced her head back and kissed her. She didn't respond like women usually did so he kissed her harder, jamming his tongue deep into her mouth. She tried to pull away but he bore down on her even harder, grinding against her. As he let go of one shoulder and groped at her breast, she broke free and ran into the kitchen.

He followed her and grabbed her again. He forced her down onto the table, unzipped his jeans and managed to rip off her panties. He used his muscular legs to pry her thighs apart. He jammed into her, hard, surprised at how tight she felt. He heard her gasp with pain and jammed into her again and again, knowing that soon she'd come around and gasp with pleasure. He ignored her sobs and struggles and, grunting with his own effort, he fucked her until he was spent.

When he was sated, he pulled out. He was satisfied and he glanced down at Starlynne's face. He stared at her in surprise. Usually when he met the eyes of a lover, he saw gratitude, satisfaction, pleasure. He always made the chicks happy, but Starlynne was sobbing, making no sound, her chest heaving and tears streaming from the corners of her eyes.

"Hey what's the matter with you?" he asked. "Oh, I get it, the first time is always hard, but look, Honey, you were fine, just fine. With a little practice you'll be great."

"Get out!" Starlynne yelled as she sat up. "You ruined me, now, get out!"

Dennis looked surprised, "Hey, what do you mean, ruined you? You can't tell me you didn't want it. Hell, Starlynne, everybody wants it."

She stared at him, wide-eyed, then jumped off the table. "You think I wanted to be raped?" she hissed, reaching into a drawer and pulling out a long, sharp, serrated knife. "Get out before I kill you!"

"Rape?" Dennis was shocked. "You think I raped you? Hell, Honey, you are nuts. I don't take anything that isn't offered. You've been giving me those sideways looks. I know when a woman wants me!"

Starlynne let out a blood-curdling scream and lunged at him with the knife.

Dennis grabbed her wrists and squeezed. As her grip loosened on the weapon, he took it from her. "Look Starlynne, I'm not into this kind of thing."

He grinned at the girl and wagged the knife like an admonishing finger. "If you're a good girl, I won't tell Ronny you like it rough."

Starlynne charged again, baring her nails, going for his eyes. Without thinking, he shoved her away, forgetting about the knife in his hand. He stared at her as she stumbled back, as she stared down at herself, at the spreading stain of red on her chest.

He'd accidentally stabbed her!

He looked at the knife, covered with her blood, then back to her. Between her onrush and his shove, he'd stabbed her in the chest. No, wait, he thought quickly, she had stabbed herself, yeah, she'd done all this to herself! She had rushed onto the glistening blade. I didn't do a damned thing wrong!

She stood there in front of him, swaying, "Help... me," she whispered as she folded to her knees. She tried to stop the bleeding, clutching at her chest, but the blood continued to spread. "Help me, I... I can't stop it... you ruined me. The... the rape..."

He thought about helping. He was trying to decide what to do, how to explain this to the authorities, but her words froze him. She was still trying to accuse him of rape! He watched her as she sank lower and fell over on her side. He stood there doing nothing as the word rape echoed in his head. He watched as she lay on the wooden floor in a spreading pool of blood. He stood above her, mesmerized, as her chest heaved with each breath she struggled to take.

This can't be happening, he thought, not to me! "

Dennis started pacing back and forth, wondering what he was going to do. He knew it was a sick accident, but he was a stranger here. How was he going to explain this when she was trying to ruin his life?

"This was supposed to be a vacation," he mumbled. "God, I'm supposed to go to law school after next year."

He had to get rid of her. Yeah, deep in the woods. With a history like hers, a mysterious disappearance would only add to the folklore. All he had to do was get rid of her.

He scooped up his bloody burden and carried her into the woods. When he was deep into the forest, he dropped her in a small clearing. She was still breathing, still watching him. "Please!" she gasped. "Don't leave me!"

He turned, ran all the way back to her place and washed off the blood. There was so much it took a long time.

Afterward, he hid the knife in his car, grabbed a shovel and ran back into the woods. She was still breathing, still conscious, but so weak she couldn't move or speak. He wanted to say something, explain to her that he had to do this, had to protect himself, but couldn't find the words. Instead he dug a hole and buried her. After all, he was sure she was dying anyway. It was dark and he worked under the light of the almost full moon.

Suddenly, he became aware he was being watched. He could feel eyes on him. He finished filling the hole, threw down the shovel and rushed away from the grave and the watching eyes. He knew it had to be an animal and yet... and yet, he hurried to get back to his car.

He sat behind the steering wheel of his locked car and tried to think things out. He was covered in blood; he'd been gone for hours, what would he tell Ronny?

An idea hit him and he took the knife out of the glove compartment. He clamped his teeth and sliced his forehead, his shoulder and his arm. The cuts were slight, but bloody. He tossed the knife into Starlynne's garden and then drove about a mile down the dirt road. He fastened his seatbelt, closed his eyes and grasping the steering wheel in a white knuckled grip, then drove off the road into the trees.

The car bounced and jerked and, with a metallic crunch, stopped. He was shaken up but not hurt. He let out the breath he'd been holding and, ignoring the burning sting of the cuts, walked back to Ronny's cabin.

Ronny was horrified. "It's all my fault, the day was too tiring. You never should have gone out again."

"No, Ron," Dennis said, cleaning his cuts. "It's just an accident."

"I'll go get Starlynne, she'll heal you!"

Dennis turned fast and snapped, "Oh no, don't bother her. I'm all right, they're only slight cuts, see?"

Ronny grew pale.

"Oops, sorry." Dennis said. "I didn't mean to make you sick. Go lie down."

Ronny did. Late night settled in on them like a heavy, dark blanket but Dennis found he couldn't sleep. About five a.m. he heard Ronny get up.

"Hey buddy, where you going? It's the middle of the night."

"Starlynne needs me. She's hurt."

"Come on, man," Dennis said, wondering how Ronny could know anything. "You're dreaming. Go back to bed."

Ronny suddenly looked at Dennis with slitted eyes. He shook his head and said, "All right. Good night."

A few minutes later Dennis heard the door open and then footsteps outside. Ronny had gone out after all.

Dennis jumped out of bed and followed Ronny as he cut through the woods to Starlynne's. Ronny started up the steps and then stopped. Dennis hid in the garden, saw the knife glittering in the waning moonlight and picked it up. He didn't want Ronny finding it.

Suddenly Ronny turned around and hurried into the forest. Dennis didn't really understand how, but he knew that Ronny was going to Starlynne.

A he thought, Ronny headed straight for the grave. He stopped before it and in the dim, dawn light, Dennis saw an unbelievable sight. There, where he had buried her body, there were flowers. Hundreds of tiny, bell-shaped flowers growing in the shape of a human. A small human about the size of Starlynne.

Ronny sank to his knees and wept.

"I didn't do it on purpose, Ron," Dennis said, coming up behind him. "It was an accident."

Ronny turned, "You raped her, took away her healing powers and she's dead! She didn't have to die. You could have saved her." Ronny jumped up

191

and tackled him to the ground.   "Damn you, Dennis," he cried, putting a stranglehold to Dennis' throat. "Damn you to Hell. You murdered her!"

Dennis shoved Ronny back, trying to break the grip on his windpipe. Ronny suddenly had the power of a weight lifter. Dennis' air was cut off. With desperation Dennis drove the knife he had forgotten he was holding into Ronny's chest. Both men grunted as blood tricked down the knife handle and down Dennis' arm. He lay there for a moment, too stunned by what he had done.

Ronny was dead. Dennis looked into his unseeing eyes. Revulsion pumped adrenaline through him, washing away the shock. He sat up quickly, pushed the corpse off him and bellowed with frustration.

"Things like this don't happen to real people!" he screamed as he staggered away from the body.

"Starlynne was right, I am a killer! No, I'm not. I'm not bad, I'm not! I didn't do anything but react! They both did this to themselves! I'm not bad!" Dennis paced like a wild man and babbled hysterically. "I'm the victim here, yeah, that's right, me. Well, I'll show them, yeah, I'll make sure no one ever knows about this!"

Dennis ran over to Starlynne's grave, fell to his knees and started pulling out all those damned little flowers. "Grow back all you want, you little bastards. No one will ever see you," he mumbled wildly, yanking out handfuls of the wildflowers and flinging them away. "These flowers aren't going to cause me any trouble, nope. They can grow back till hell freezes over. I'll keep ripping them out. Starlynne, you're dead and you're gonna stay buried!"

He jumped up, grabbed the shovel he'd thrown down earlier and buried Ronny next to Starlynne. "Well, Ronny, you said you wanted to be with her forever," he mumbled, laughing at the irony of it all. "Now you have your chance."

The sun wasn't quite up when he finished. The horse-flies were starting to buzz around his head and sweat was forming at his hairline. The bushes to his right were rustling and he saw a shadowy shape moving deeper into the thick woods.

"Hey," he yelled. "Hey you! Come back here!" He dropped the shovel and ran after the witness. "Christ, Oh God, somebody saw me! Please God, don't make me have to kill anyone else. Please!" He pushed his way through thick brush and brambles, tearing his clothes and cutting his skin. He had to find that witness.

He felt chilled goose-bumps on his arms and the hair on the back of his neck tingled. He stopped and looked around. He saw trees, just trees. And yet... he was being watched again. He was now the one on the defensive. Shuddering, he turned and ran back through the woods, back to the clearing.

He was panting, his chest aching when he was stopped by a sound. A voice calling his name. "Dennis, Dennis, Dennis," the words repeated, then added, "Buried alive... bleed to death... murder."

"Show yourself, you bastard!" Dennis screamed at the dark woods surrounding him. "Tell me what you want! Goddamnit, I've said I'm sorry! It wasn't murder, I had no choice!"

He saw movement, a figure at the edge of the trees. They were all going to have to leave him alone, he thought. He had to make Ronny and Starlynne understand that it was all a horrible accident. He had to make them leave him alone.

The sun was up and in the pink glow of dawn he saw those tiny white bells back over Starlynne's grave and a heartier yellow blossom covering the shape of Ronny. Their flowery arms were outstretched, hands joined.

Dennis stepped over to the graves and looked down, then over at the man shape at the edge of the woods. "Who are you?"

As if in answer, vines slithered out from the flowers and twisted around Dennis' feet and legs, rooting him to the spot. "Hey," he bellowed, struggling against the plants. "Let go!" He pulled, tried to lift his feet, but couldn't break free.

The witness left the trees and approached. "Who are you?" Dennis screamed, knees weak, heart pounding wildly. He searched in vain for a chance to get away. He went to grab the vines but discovered they were full of thorns.

The figure neared and Dennis saw it wasn't quite human. He stared with absolute terror at the bat-like wings and hoof feet. He fell backwards, the vines pinning his feet to the ground. "Who the hell are you?" he shrieked, knowing it was futile.

The creature stopped in front of him and silently looked toward the flower-covered bodies. Then it reached for him and answered in a gravelly voice, "Just a friend of the family."

Where The Wounded Trees Wait
Paul Edwards

Dedicated to the memory of William "Billy"
Edwards
11/11/1908 – 31/08/1991

Introduction

Iesu! Cyfaill f'enaid cu!

Iesu, cyfaill f'enaid cu,
I dy fynwes gad im' ffoi.
Tra bo'r dyfroedd o bob tu,
A'r ym tymhestloedd yn crynhoi.
Cudd fi, O fy Mhrynwr! cudd,
Nes 'r el heibio'r storom gref;
Yn arweinydd imi bydd
Nes im' dd'od i dyernas nef.
Noddfa arall gwn nid oes,
Ond Tydi i'm henaid gwan;
Ti, fu farw ar a groes
Yw fy nghymorth yn mhob man;
Ynot, O fy Iesu! mae
Holl ymddiried f'enaid byw:
nerth rho imi i barhau,
Nes dod adref, at fy Nuw.
Pob peth ynot, Iesu, mae;

Mwy na phopeth ynot sydd;
Cyfod Di'r syrthiedig rai,
Ac i'r cleifion meddyg bydd;
I'r gwangalon cysur rho,
Deillion tywys yn dy ffyrdd;
Ninnau yn dragyddol rown
Ar dy ben fendithion fyrdd.
Gras sydd ynot fel y mor,
Gras i faddeu fy holl fai;
Boed i'w ffrydiau, Arglwydd Iôr!
Oddi wrth bechod fy nglanhau;
Ffynnon bywyd f'enaid gwiw,
Rhydd im' gysur ar fy nhaith,
Llona f'ysbryd tra b'wyf byw,
Tardd i dragwyddoldeb maith!

(Welsh soldiers sang 'Jesus, Lover Of My Soul' to composer Joseph Parry's tune, 'Aberystwyth', before going into battle at Mametz in 1916. The words represent a deep, heartfelt calling on God to provide, if not protection physically, then at least the courage to face whatever may lie ahead.)

***

"You have it..." the old woman reached out, touching the crown of the child's head, "...but don't be frightened – it's a gift! That's what your grandfather believed, anyway." She took her hand away, tilting her head to the side and smiling. "I've

197

only been able to look back. Perhaps it's the same for you… although it's more than scrying, remember? And it's important to talk; not to brush it under the carpet and pretend it's not there. What hope do we have if we don't talk about it, if we don't try and understand?"

Her fingers brushed the child's face, as light as feathers. "When I was your age," she sighed, "I couldn't read a book without having to scan the last few pages first. I had to be sure there was a happy ending, see." She shook her head, chuckled to herself. "But I've learnt to let the future be." Her eyes clouded suddenly and for a moment or two she was miles away, locked in some other world, some other time completely. Then, blinking twice, refocusing, added: "I think I knew, in my heart of hearts, what would happen. Perhaps I should have tried harder… Maybe there could have been some way of…preventing it." A deep frown joined her eyebrows together. "But whenever I scry, I discern loops and terrible dark patterns…"

Her fingers slipped away from the child, and a powerful silence enfolded them both.

The child gazed at the woman's troubled expression, no longer feeling quite so alone.

Chapter I

28 Years Later

She walked barefoot toward the gaunt skeletons of the trees. Mud splashed and squelched, squishing up between her toes, spattering the backs of her legs. All around the land was an eerie nightscape of smoking craters, dead bodies, broken picket posts and barbed wire. Some men, still alive, mortally wounded, were crying out and begging for water. Some plucked at her legs as she went by.

In blasted shell holes she saw men who'd had limbs blown off and others who, having been shot, had crawled in from the machine gun fire to die. She scanned each face, looking for him, but couldn't make him out, couldn't see him yet.

Horror and frustration threatened to overwhelm her. A fusilier with half his head blown away lay against his machine gun, hand still on the trigger. Another was kneeling close to the wood, a red trickle creeping from his bayonetted throat. To her left, a young man was running in wild circles, shrieking, his mind clearly broken by war.

The wood loomed, all light shrinking away suddenly, unnaturally. The trees were calling for her, she thought. Beckoning her in. Wanting her for their own. "We gravitate together," she breathed. "It's what we do."

Lumps of flesh hung over branches like discoloured rags. Decapitated heads gazed up with glassy, soulless eyes. A human hand crouched in a bisected tree trunk like a pale grotesque spider.

Then the trees were moving, waving in a strange, hypnotic fashion, their branches reaching down slowly, mesmerizingly, enfolding her like they were arms, holding her close, still and tight. In the blink of an eye they were arms – sinewy and stripped of flesh, dripping blood on the leaves and twigs scattered around her.

She closed her eyes as they eased her to the ground, a weird sense of serenity descending as she hugged them back, easing her racing heart and reeling mind.

And then, for the first time since she could remember, before she would wake up, choking and gasping, she felt at peace, whole.

***

I do not want to die out here alone…

Huw's words ghosted through Caryl's head as she sat patiently at the table, eyes fastened on the clock on the wall. She felt unusually calm, focused and ready for scrying.

Gene's hand slid into his pocket, fidgeting with an object. His gaze drifted from her face, fixing itself on some indeterminable spot above her shoulder.

"How will you…? he began, then dropped his gaze to his knees, pensive and silent. Moments later, he looked up and tried again. "Do you know exactly…?" He shook his head, defeated.

The waiter came over with a bottle of Côtes du Rhône, showing Caryl the label. He uncorked it, poured a small amount into Caryl's glass.

She sipped. "C'est bon."

"Aimez-vous?"

"Oui, c'est très bien."

The waiter smiled, nodded and filled their glasses before moving on to the next table.

Caryl ran a finger around the rim of her wine glass. "I'm here. We're actually here, Gene."

The crimson light of the swiftly setting sun trailed through the windows, spilling slanted beams across the table top and floor.

"I'm glad you came," she said, reaching out, stroking his knuckles. "I didn't think you would."

It was a conscious change of tack. She'd grown increasingly aware over the past few days that she'd been irritable and dismissive of him. Anxiety had been bubbling up, clawing for release.

"It is pretty here," Gene conceded. "Quiet, though. Perhaps a little too quiet for my taste."

She knew he had an agenda; business of his own. He was waiting for the right time to broach it, she supposed. Whatever it was that he wanted to say, she hoped he wouldn't raise it here, at the table, because all she wanted to talk about was scrying.

Fleetingly she thought of Jake and how he'd talk incessantly and passionately, about everything and anything, it seemed. They were chalk and cheese, Gene and Jake. Couldn't be more different if they tried.

A week ago, she'd slept with Jake again. She'd promised herself that she wouldn't do it, but she fell under his spell and spent the night at his. In his bed, he'd made the usual idle promises, whilst listing reasons why her relationship with Gene would fail.

The waiter reappeared, setting their main courses down in front of them.

"The battlefield's about a mile from here." She threw a hopeful glance at Gene. "Perhaps we could go for a walk after supper?"

"Must be like looking for a needle in a haystack."

"Think I've pinpointed it, thanks to Nan's efforts over the years."

Gene thanked the departing waiter, then puffed out his cheeks and sighed.

What did this mean to him, if anything, she wondered? Could he imagine himself here, seventy-two years ago, crouched in a trench, miles from home and knowing that he could die, at any given moment, far from everyone and everything he loved?

She set her cutlery down, reached under the table for her rucksack and opened it. Maybe this would make it real, she thought, taking out the photograph, passing it to him.

He put his fork down and studied the photograph.

She knew the picture like the back of her hand. Huw, in his 1902 Pattern Service Dress tunic, trousers and hat. He'd a kind, compassionate face and eyes that seemed to convey a message which she couldn't quite decipher.

The photo was old and brittle. The thought of it perishing someday distressed her. "I think you look like your Nan," he said, handing the photograph back. "You, your Mum; your Nan. You all look the same." He picked his fork back up and resumed eating. "You should smile more, Caryl. I never see you smile."

She pretended not to hear him.

Leaning across the table, teeth bared, she said, "I can find him. I know I can."

***

Excerpt from the diary of Pte Huw Price: -

6th December 1915

We set off just before five, after the carts and horses had boarded. There had been torrential rain in Southampton, so I was soaked through by the time I arrived at my berthing space on the boat.

It did not take long to find my bed - bunk numbers correspond with the number written on your billet, which is issued as you board. The bunk is comfortable enough, consisting of a strip of canvas supported by four iron uprights. At least I have a bed; some fellows here have had to make do with the floor, as there are not enough bunks to go round.

The washroom is located opposite and, as I was picking my way across the sleeping men earlier, the sway of the boat knocked me on top of one chap who made the most dreadful fuss. I apologised profusely, picked myself up and made my way to the washroom before he could wake the entire boat up.

It goes without saying that I am missing you and Sara, Siân. I am surrounded by people, yet I have never felt more alone in my life. It has made me realise how much I take for granted, and how lucky I am to have you both.

Before I left, do you remember what we talked about? That conversation we had about your gift? I firmly believe it is a gift. In fact, I envy your talent and ability to think and feel as deeply as you do.

They say you cannot know another person but believe me when I say that what I feel for you is both strong and true. You are never far from my thoughts. Sara, too. You give me purpose, a reason to live. I carry you both in my heart, no matter where I go.

Chapter II

Caryl gazed up at the dragon, which faced the wood and was tearing at barbed wire. She ran her fingers across the words carved on the plinth – MAMETZ WOOD – and sang, softly, "Llona f'ysbryd tra b'wyf byw, tardd i dragwyddoldeb maith." It was the hymn that the soldiers had sung shortly before advancing; Jesus, Lover Of My Soul to the tune of Aberystwyth.

Gene touched her elbow. She flicked open her eyes and whispered, "Think I've been here before."

Gene backed away, shoulders hunched, face in shadow, toward the information plaque opposite the sculpture. Does he know more than he lets on, she wondered? Would he dash her head against the plinth in a jealous rage?

"Which battalion was your grandfather in?" he called suddenly, a disembodied voice in the darkness.

"He was in the 16th Battalion, under the 115th Brigade." She edged toward him, mud squelching and sucking at her shoes. "A two-pronged simultaneous assault." She tucked a loose strand of hair behind her ear, then added: "Once they entered the wood, both Divisions were to advance towards the centre ride and then swing to the north, clearing the enemy as they advanced." She squinted at the plaque as she continued, "The 38th had the added task of sweeping across the southern end to clear any enemy from that locality."

"They suffered catastrophic casualties."

"More than 400 men." White mist escaped her lips, wheeling, curling in on itself. "Granddad hung on in there. Lasted until nightfall; around this time, I suppose."

"Where did they attack?"

She waved a pale hand and said, "There, to the south-east. Got as far as 200 yards."

They trudged down metal steps then started across the field together. Overhead, ragged clouds drifted across a waxing moon.

"Huw was last seen by Private Davies a couple of hundred yards from the wood." She pointed at the stark-black trees ahead, standing like sentries in the night. "He dug in, sheltering from the intense shelling and gunfire." She glanced around at the dragon, which was now just a shadow on the hilltop. "One of the last of the 115th to fall."

He nodded once but didn't reply. She'd hoped that he'd put an arm around her, or take her hand; instead, he kept his head bowed, his gaze lowered as they traipsed solemnly toward the wood.

"Around here…" She stopped suddenly, dropping her rucksack. "…he sheltered from the bombardment in a shell hole. Dug right in and held his position."

She opened her rucksack and took out Huw's diary; a jewellery box; photographs; Davies' letters. Sat quietly beside them, studying them in turn.

Gene hitched his jeans up and dropped to his haunches. "Is that everything?"

"Everything I can use." Her gaze drifted over Davies' words, a soldier who'd survived Mametz and had documented his experiences in letters to loved ones back home. Huw was mentioned, as well as other men from the 38th (Welsh) Infantry Division. Davies had described Huw's immense bravery and courage, fighting back in a shell hole before succumbing at the edge of the wood at around 2100 hours.

There were more photographs tucked inside the diary, taken by Caryl's grandmother. Each depicted the spot where they now sat, although the pictures were of the wood and field in broad daylight.

"Nan came out here in '79, '81 and '85," Caryl explained. "These were taken three years ago, in '85; the year before Nan died. Huw's diary, the letters... they helped Nan pinpoint where it was he perished."

Gene was hunched deep into his coat, hands thrust in his pockets. "How long do you think it'll take?"

"Could be a night. Maybe two. Could be a week. But I don't want to leave until..."

"Just be careful, okay? I know how it devastates you. I remember after your grandmother..." He trailed off, not needing to continue. She felt his eyes on her but couldn't meet them. Didn't need his concern now.

She examined a photograph of Huw and Siân on their wedding day, Siân dressed in a satin gown and veil; a photograph of Huw with Mum in his lap when Mum had been a baby; the picture of Huw in his full Service Dress, a hint of a smile etching his youthful face.

She touched the letters, her fingers careful not to damage those faded, brittle leaves. Closed her eyes and repeated a line from Huw's diary: "I carry you both in my heart, no matter where I go."

She opened a jewellery box, took out a lock of his hair. Nan had cut it from her husband's head just before he'd left and now, holding it up, Caryl whispered and chanted strange, esoteric words. She closed her eyes, a rushing sound filling her skull. When she opened them again, the world flickered and jumped like a trapped frame on a screen.

Keep concentrating, she thought. Keep chanting; focusing…

From the distance came the sounds of detonation; the barking of orders, warnings and commands. She kept her wide-open eyes nailed to the moon, specks dancing across her vision, flashing, jumping, flickering. She had to utilise all her senses to bring forth the past, to transport herself to where she needed to go…

She suddenly began to tremble, then her body shook in a spectacular spasm. If Gene intervened now, she'd hate him, particularly after everything she'd instructed, after everything she'd…

208

Her head rolled and the moon tumbled – a sickening white blur – and there was a hole now, a portal; a tear in reality – opening, widening; whiteness burning like a supernova at the edges of her vision...

She saw holes in the trees and flames licking around trunks. Heard shrieks and saw people – shadowy blurs – flit past and through her as she focused on anchoring herself, of solidifying herself at the scene. All around the air was filling with the rattle of machine guns and the screams of the dying. Shells howled overhead, the ground rocking beneath her feet as they exploded nearby.

There – dug into the earth not far from the wood – a collection of twisting, writhing bodies squirming through smoke... Could one be...?

The light was suddenly like a burning magnesium ribbon – and then she was back to herself, back in darkness, silence, huddled over, gasping, panting, wheezing at the ground.

Gene laid his hand on her shoulder. "Are you...?"

She vomited and he withdrew his hand quickly.

He grabbed a packet of tissues from her rucksack, dabbed the sick around her mouth. Her nose was bleeding so he cleaned that up, too. Then he scooped Siân's items up, carefully packing them back into the rucksack. "Can you walk?"

Caryl nodded desolately, got up and they trudged across the field together, back toward Mametz. She was sick once more in the hotel, retching into the toilet in their bathroom. She scraped her hair away from her face, straightened. Stared long and hard into the mirror above the sink. She was so thin; skeletal, almost. Fluorescent lighting washed over the criss-cross of self-inflicted scars on her arms. She felt Gene's eyes on them but didn't care.

"You okay?"

She padded into the room, then sat beside him on the bed. Lowering her head, she pinched tissue out of her nostrils and placed the bloodied, squashed-up balls on the bedside table.

Downstairs, a Frenchman began talking to someone; then a door closed loudly, firmly, causing silence to settle once more.

"Do you think you'll be sick again?" he asked.

"Don't think so." She laughed without humour. "Can't imagine there's much left to come out." She glanced at him. "I was close, Gene. I was right back there, you know?"

When he didn't reply, she turned on him: "Why the hell do I talk to you about it? You don't believe in anything you can't see, right?"

"Yes, I don't understand!" He was shaking now, his eyes wide, round, and blazing. "But I'm here, aren't I? Isn't that enough?"

She shook her head, wishing it was Jake here. But that could never happen, because Jake wouldn't commit. Had never shown the slightest inclination of settling down. Besides, she'd hate for him to see her like this.

She held up her trembling arms, gaze dancing over the scars on her flesh. "I don't deserve to be here."

"Caryl…"

"Let me finish." She fixed him with a glare. "I mean, what am I? Really? What have I achieved?" She mumbled to herself, drawing the back of her hand across her eyes. "It's the guilt that eats me, you know? I'm a fucking waste of time and space. That's why this is important – I've got to give something back." Her hands dropped limply in her lap, her fingers flexing, furling. "It's the living that scares me, Gene."

"I know." He gripped her shoulder, then squeezed. "But I think this brings you down. It's a curse…" he trailed off, seemingly unsure as to whether to continue or not.

She sat dead still, mulling over his words.

"I think you need to rest," he said at last. "You'll feel better in the morning."

"Don't fucking patronise me."

"I'm not…"

She shot up, walked to the other side of the bed and dragged back the duvet. Crawled into bed and pressed herself against the wall with her back to him, silent and still. He groaned, undressed and climbed into bed with her.

His arm hesitantly snaked around her body to squeeze and hold her tight. It was the first time he'd held her since they'd arrived. She thought about the last thing Jake had said, in a café before she'd gone to France: "We'll come back to each other. We gravitate together, it's what we do."

She twisted onto her back, lost herself to silence. Soon, Gene began to snore. She stared at the ceiling, feeling empty, a melee of thoughts churning in her mind...

Thick, smoggy darkness descended.

Out of the darkness came hollered orders, warnings and commands.

The wood loomed, flashing a deep, ominous red. Tongues of flame flickered between tree trunks. Severed heads and lumps of flesh hung in the claws of splintered branches. Mangled corpses in khaki and field grey lay in a smouldering crater, frightfully mutilated, one lad decapitated by a shell, just as if he'd been guillotined. Everywhere the ground was littered with broken guns, bayonets, shells and men.

Smoke poured forth from the trees, fierce and black, almost obscuring all vision, its acrid stench filling Caryl's nostrils and clawing at her throat. Struggling to breathe, to see, she tried to focus on a man who'd turned briefly, fleetingly, in her direction.

Realisation hit her...

She staggered forwards, shouting and shrieking Huw's name.

Machine guns roared.

Screams erupted.

Shells whistled.

She was almost in arm's reach, but still he didn't turn; still didn't react. Smoke drove into her eyes, blinding her. Then, seeing him again, she grit her teeth and ploughed on, almost falling, tripping, arm outstretched, fingers moving…

"Caryl!"

Gene was leaning over her, his eyes bulging white circles in the shadows across his face. "Caryl, you okay?" His voice quietened, softened. "You were crying out in your sleep again."

She barely heard his words, his voice. Her hand slipped from his shoulder and she rolled over, away from him, choking and weeping bitter tears until sleep claimed her once more.

***

Excerpts from the diary of Pte Huw Price: -

30th December 1915

It has not stopped raining for two days straight. The trenches are ankle deep – some places calf deep – in mud and in other places there are rushing streams of foul-smelling brown water.

We spend most of our time displacing the mud, either by filling sandbags or piling it up into a wall and beating it into a firm rampart.

Rats surround us – last night they were all over me, scrabbling after the rations in my haversack.

When they scurried close to my face, I leapt up, cursing and spitting, searching the trench for another spot to lie down in.

The days bleed into each other and nothing seems to change. Fear, boredom, boredom, fear — they swing from one to another and we are all so tired we can barely think straight.

Sleep is welcome respite and in my dreams I see you, Siân – as clear as anything! Are you working your magic, my love? Are you reaching out, comforting me through your talent, your gift? I strongly believe that you are; that our minds are meeting... It is what gets me through these long, difficult days. I see you in dreams. I talk to you -- I hear your voice!

5th January 1916

Blwyddyn Newydd Dda! Nothing new to report in Laventie – the drudgery of trench life continues, although the weather has been kinder to us these past few days.

Siân – this might sound crazy, but sometimes I really do believe that you are here, beside me, in these cold, filthy trenches. I know that you are close; my dreams are lucid, vivid and I hear and see you all so clearly.

4th April 1916

I believe we will be moving soon, manning the front in Nord-Pas-de-Calais. We have certainly had our turn at the drudgery of the trenches. The months have been monotonous, with little change occurring and each day very much like the last.

I have become resigned to my time out here but I have to say that nothing we are made to do gives us any feeling of resentment. We know we have a job to do and we have become like brothers, fond of our country and each other.

When we are reunited, I shall look back on the rats, the trenches, the lice, the mud and the rain and bask in the fact that I am with you, Siân. Each night I lie on the floor of the trench and tell myself that I am strong, because I have gone one more day without you.

Chapter III

The sun cut through the windowpanes, assailing Caryl with its long, slanting arrows of light. She wore shades and was nursing a cup of black, bitter coffee.

"Not hungry?" Gene sliced open his croissant with a butter knife.

She shook her head, averting her gaze toward the breakfast bar. Last night's dream lingered, making her feel queasy and unwell. She'd dreamt something else, too; something about being cradled in the arms of trees, blood dripping from their stripped, flayed bark.

Gene was reading The Daily Mirror, a newspaper she loathed. He'd grabbed a copy from the rack when they'd come down for breakfast earlier. It was yesterday's edition, but at least it was in English, at least it was familiar. It seemed to have made his morning.

"You all right?" He lifted his face and scowled. "I wish you'd take those glasses off."

"Wish you hadn't chosen to sit in the sun like this."

"We can move." He gestured with a listless flick of his hand. "There's a free table over there."

"It's fine." She frowned and firmed her jaw. "Got a headache."

He grunted, tutted, then said: "Don't think it's a good idea you trying this evening." She leaned back in her seat, arms tightly folded across her chest. "You need recovery time. A chance to heal, Caryl."

Anger flared within her. "The whole point of me being here…"

"I know, I know." His raised both hands in a placating gesture. "But it's dangerous, and I can see…"

"Don't want to talk about it."

Blood rose to his face, silencing him. He pushed his plate away, muttering to himself.

Had he failed to grasp the importance of this trip? She doubted he'd the imagination to understand the living hell people like Huw went through – men who sacrificed their freedom so that their children and grandchildren could enjoy theirs.

He pushed the last of his croissant into his mouth, then mumbled, "Going for a smoke. Coming?"

They stood outside in the garden beside the rhododendrons, a sudden breeze feeling like warm breath on her skin. "Sure I saw him," she said at last, her anger slipping away. "He was lying in a shell hole, dug right in. The dead scattered around him."

He pulled on his cigarette, eyes squinting into slits. "You don't have to rush this. We have the room for a week, and…"

"It's better on a full moon, remember? And the forecast's good."

They started walking alongside the hotel, following a gravelled path to the front of the building. Mametz's streets were quiet; there was hardly any traffic on the road. They passed the signs pointing the way to the Welsh memorial and Dantzig Alley British Cemetery. Gene flicked his cigarette to the ground, stopped and stomped it into the gravel.

Caryl was thirty-eight, and growing increasingly aware of her own mortality. These days, she felt fragile – desperately afraid of everything and anything, it seemed. She didn't know what she wanted; wasn't sure of anything anymore.

She knew that life wasn't long and that the window of opportunity was fleeting; precious. Sometimes, she could hear the sand falling in her own personal hourglass. Could feel the window shrinking, the darkness closing in...

She'd heard the phrase "You can never truly know a person" many times, but a desperate part of her wanted that to be untrue. She glanced at Gene, wondering what hopes and dreams he harboured. It was disturbing putting herself in his shoes, knowing what she knew about herself. Knowing how she felt about him; how she felt about Jake.

The way his face was twitching suggested that he was building up to something. Whatever it was, it had been there since their visit to her parents' house in March.

"I found Mametz Wood eerie," he said suddenly, snapping her from her thoughts.

She absently rubbed her hands together. "It's an eerie place," she agreed.

They perched on a bench beside a life-sized bronze statue of a soldier. Gene reached into his coat pocket, pulled out his Marlboros. Slotted a cigarette into his mouth and offered one to Caryl. She shook her head, glancing at the soldier standing sternly over them.

"Shortly before we left," he said, "I did some research of my own. Found out how some of these hard-nosed army types admitted to seeing some pretty weird stuff in Mametz Wood."

She watched him light his cigarette, then suggested, "Perhaps they have a little of what I have."

"Visitors had the sensation of being watched – feeling dozens of eyes on them as they've explored the wood. There's been reports of bugle calls; the ghostly sounds of battle re-enactment...

"There's this one account," he sniffed, breathing smoke out of his nostrils, "where this guy saw a girl in Mametz Wood, lying there slumped against a tree, a sort of relieved smile on her face. Which doesn't make any sense, but anyway..." He gazed at the cigarette smouldering between his fingers. "The guy shouted and then she just vanished... as if into thin air." He grabbed his coat collar, pulled it close. "That one stood out, amongst the usual soldier and orb sightings." He shrugged.

219

"Don't know why, but I read up on a lot of supernatural stuff before coming out here. Not usually a fan of ghost stories and such."

"I believe the past wants to be reawakened," she said quietly, urgently. "I feel it calling, Gene. In my subconscious; my dreams." Her gaze dropped, she stared into space. Then, shaking her head, looking up: "I felt connected to the wood... like I'd been there before, you know? And I felt a presence, pulling me, trying to drive me among the trees. It was so close, I could almost touch it. But I was afraid of it, too."

His eyes drifted over the shutters across the windows of the hotel opposite. "Maybe it's not something to be frightened of," he mused. "Perhaps it's... good. Harmonious, even." He chuckled, shrugged, drew on his cigarette. "Perhaps it didn't come from the past, whatever it was that came to you like that back there."

He got to his feet, flicked his cigarette to the floor. Ground it out with the heel of his shoe. She rubbed her arms, recalling that dream where the branches had grabbed her, holding her still, close and tight.

"I'd like to walk over to the cemetery this afternoon," she said. "Nan thought he might have been buried there, although his name isn't in the register. His name's etched on the Memorial to the Missing at Thiepval, though."

"The cemetery's just along here?" He gestured in the direction of the road.

"Yes. Just a short walk."

He nodded. That was sealed, then.

***

Excerpts from the diary of Pte Huw Price: -

4th June 1916

I saw my first dead body today. His name had been Hughes, shot to pieces at his post in the trench we dug yesterday. Found by Fritz while we were on reconnaissance. His body was riddled with holes and with his innocent, almost serene expression, he looked little more than a boy who had laid down and fallen asleep with his eyes open. I got thinking then… At the end, had he been scared? Calm? Had he known what was about to happen? Did he have family? He died here alone without comfort or companionship. No one is born alone and no one should die alone.

The others dug his grave while I prepared the body. I found a photograph in his coat of a pretty girl with long dark hair. Could he have loved the girl as deeply as I love you, Siân? How cruel and sad that he should be denied a life with her.

I wrapped the body in oil skin, then we buried him, each taking turns to say a few words. As the first shovelfuls of dirt landed, the selfish thought of this could have been me could not be helped by my aching heart.

After we had finished, we feared another German assault, so we kept constant obs throughout the night, although orders to pursue the Germans in the morning filled me with both excitement and dread.

5th June 1916

I killed a man – what a truly sickening thing for me to have to write. If only you were here to talk to, Siân; I am scared of what I am becoming out here.

It happened this afternoon, on the outskirts of Festubert. We had been drifting to the west, having almost given up our pursuit of Fritz. Then we saw them – clad in grey tunics, coats and caps – running for the cover of the trees. There were five in total and they knew we were on to them.

It has been raining heavily so visibility was poor. Nonetheless, we aimed and let go, the German patrol dispersing under a hail of our bullets. I was thinking of Hughes as I went after one man, who was sprinting toward a chapel on the side of a road. I thought of the praise I would get if I shot him, although my excitement was tempered by the most awful fear imaginable.

The German reached the chapel and was just about to push through when he looked around – that was when I crouched, took aim and let go, dropping the man with a single shot from my rifle.

I felt elated, euphoric; Lewis reached my side, gripping my shoulder and shaking me, grinning: "Well done, well done."

The other chaps joined us, patting my cheek and commending me for my efforts. Then, straightening, ever-watchful, we made our way toward the chapel with the rain lashing down hard around us.

We reached the building and the man's motionless body. Dowie kicked the German, but he did not move, did not respond. We were satisfied that he was dead. Lewis pushed open the door and we all peered inside. There was nobody within, just a lot of dust and debris cluttering the floor. We focused our attentions on the soldier, turning him over and gazing into his face. His cap was off, his short blond hair spattered with mud and soil. I crouched and searched his coat. In one of the pockets I found a small bible, well-thumbed and torn at the edges.

Written on the fly-leaf in a child's handwriting was the single word Dada.

The men were quick to heap their praises and compliments on me, but the euphoria passed and was quickly replaced by a numbness and a sense of regret, over what I had done.

We held position for a couple of hours, waiting to see if the Germans would return. Then, at last, we gave up and marched on to Givenchy, cold, tired, and wet. All the while, I could not shake the dead soldier's face, or the bible with the child's handwriting in, out of my head. I kept thinking that somewhere in that soldier's fatherland was a little child who called him "Dada."

6th June 1916

Siân, how I wish I could talk to you – you realise how much you truly miss someone when something happens, good or bad, and the one person you want to tell is the person who is not there.

I had a nightmare last night. I was trying to find you, but it was so densely dark and foggy that I could not make you out at all. I remember feeling horribly disorientated as I called out your name, but I do not think you ever heard me.

This ties in with a feeling that I have had since leaving Laventie; a silly notion really, but it nags away all the same. I keep thinking that something bad is going to happen to me. I hope you do not think me paranoid, it is just the way I have been feeling. Hopefully, I will read back on this someday and laugh, although it is strange... It's like something bad has happened, but it just hasn't reached me yet. Whatever it is, it's coming... and I am just not ready for it. I mean, to let go. I am not making any sense here; I am weary and confused, weighed down by worry and fatigue all the time.

I try and visualise your face in the darkness, but all I see is Hughes' face, or the dead German's.

Why do I not dream of you now? Just thinking about it fills me with such tremendous sadness.

The trench is quiet and the other chaps sound asleep. One of the sandbags has split and I hear soil pattering the ground – a slow, sibilant hiss. It keeps distracting my train of thought, setting my nerves on edge. It has awakened something inside that I cannot quite describe but frightens me, nonetheless.

Chapter IV

They pushed through the gate and entered Dantzig Alley British Cemetery. At the end of the grounds rose a cross, THEIR NAME LIVETH FOR EVERMORE chiselled on its base. Flowers and wreaths lay scattered around it.

Caryl picked up the Cemetery Register, vainly searching its pages for Huw. As Nan'd said, his name wasn't there, despite this being the most likely place for him to have been buried.

Caryl raised her sunglasses, swiftly rubbed her eyes. The sudden surge of emotion made her want to tell Gene everything, freeing herself of guilt. She sniffed, pushed her glasses up. No. If there was a time, it wasn't now.

Jake knew about Gene, Gene didn't know about Jake. Jake had been in and out of her life since she was nineteen; they'd got together shortly after college and were together five years. She'd been with Gene for eighteen months now and he was the only boyfriend she'd ever introduced her parents to. He was practical, pragmatic and conservative; she knew right away that they'd approve.

But, after introducing him to her parents, their inevitable approval had troubled and disturbed her immensely. For days afterwards, she'd seriously considered breaking up with him, just to spite her father and mother.

Her issues with her parents were complex, their approval of Gene rousing a rebellious streak that had long been dormant.

"Caryl?" Gene placed a hand on her arm, shaking it, causing her to start and blink out of her thoughts. She glanced at the information board he'd been studying. "This is now the final resting place of over 2,000 servicemen," he read aloud, "of whom some 500 remain unidentified."

Her eyes ghosted over the unnamed graves beside them, the simple words A SOLDIER OF THE GREAT WAR chiselled on the headstones.

"I'll find you," Caryl breathed. "I'll show you how you endured."

They turned and wandered the grounds, trees rustling around them. Gene tugged her sleeve, flashed her an uneasy smile. "Shall we go?"

Caryl's head was filled with Nan and Huw as they followed the road back to Mametz. There was barely any light in the sky, despite the time of year. Great grey swathes of cloud gathered ominously, threatening rain.

They didn't go straight to the hotel, choosing to visit a café instead. It was small and quiet, only a few people inside at round rickety tables and in the armchairs. They chose a table in the corner, near the bar. The wallpaper was patterned with what looked like entwining branches, snaking and swirling around each other into insane designs. Twisting, circling, they swallowed themselves like the Ouroboros. Caryl took off her sunglasses, laid them on the table. Massaged her brow with her fingers in slow, circular motions.

As Gene ordered coffees, she visualised her visit to Nan's house in March. Nan's furniture had still been there; hadn't been moved or packed up yet. She had chosen a spot on the carpet, Caryl had sat down and spread Nan's belongings out in front of her – photographs; a doll that Nan had owned since childhood; Nan's satin wedding gown and veil; diaries Nan'd kept that documented her scrying. From the diaries, Caryl had gleaned how supportive Huw had been, helping Siân cope with the nightmares and hallucinations she'd endured. He'd been her rock, her constant. When he'd died, Nan'd lost everything.

Caryl hadn't needed much as there'd been plenty of Nan around – skin flakes sifting through the air or gathered upon surfaces throughout the room. She'd uttered the arcane words, spells; used the moon through the window to create the bridge, the tunnel, back to another day, another time completely.

The sudden sight of Nan had been shocking – curled up like a question mark in her chair, her arms folded, fingers gripping scrawny shoulders, wrinkled, yellow flesh wrapping brittle bones like clingfilm.

"Nan…" Caryl had said her name, over and over, trying to get an acknowledgment, a reaction. "Nan, I'm here. It's me, Caryl."

Siân's eyes had cleared of fog – and Caryl had taken the chance, saying all that she'd needed to say, hoping to provide comfort, hope, and reassurance in Nan's last moments.

Gene sat down, breaking her reverie. "Ordered us Cappuccinos."

She picked up her glasses, pushed them back on her face. Drew back the sleeve of her jacket and stroked the scars on her arm.

"You know what Mum said about Nan," she frowned, "after Nan'd died?"

Gene contemplated this for a moment. "No," he said at last.

"She said it was the lunacy that got her. That it broke her mind, like everybody knew it would." She paused to allow silence, then added: "Said this in front of me. Despite knowing that I have this...thing; this so-called 'gift'." A deep scowl momentarily contorted her features. "Mum was fortunate, see. It skipped a generation, missing her out completely."

"Caryl." He drummed his fingers on the tabletop. "They worry about you, that's all."

She twisted her face away. "I'm a problem that they can't fix. They're exasperated by me."

The waiter put their coffees down along with the bill, then turned and headed for the bar again.

"Is that how you see yourself?" Gene gingerly softened his voice. "A problem that needs fixing?"

"Why do you feel the need to defend them all the time?"

He heaved an exaggerated sigh. "I think they worry about you, that's all. They feel like there's a barrier up, which they can't break through."

She shook her head, muttered under her breath.

"I chatted with your Mum when we saw them last."

"Talking about me behind my back, were you?"

"It wasn't like that." He leaned back in his seat, frowning. "It made me realise that bridges need to be built. I mean, she cares for you; very much so. Your father, too. They think it's great that you were close to Siân. That you're so locked in your family's history. Sara never had much of a relationship with Siân, who never stopped grieving after your grandfather died." He shuffled forward, the chair legs squeaking. "Your mother felt the impact of that, I think. Having to live in the shadow of her grief. And don't forget, Sara was denied a father – that must have been hard, growing up without knowing him. But your mother was never jealous of your relationship with Siân. In fact, she was grateful." He allowed for a moment's pause before adding: "It was obvious that you were struggling."

Her fingers slipped away from her scars.

She recalled sitting in the kitchen of her parents' house in February, going through some of Nan's personal artefacts in cardboard boxes. They'd come across Siân's wedding ring; the one

Huw had chosen for her, with its diamond and two sapphires.

"You can't take that," Mum'd said quickly, exchanging a glance with Gene; a peculiar look that had unsettled Caryl greatly.

Jake surfaced in her mind again. She wanted him, that's what this was about, really. But Jake had let her down, time and time again. She didn't think he could change. Perhaps it was time to let go; to forget him and move on at last.

They finished their coffees, settled the bill with the waiter. Left the café and crossed the road toward the waiting hotel. The dark clouds had shifted and the sky was blue, the sun warm and bright. They sat beside each other on rusted chairs, in the patioed area outside the conservatory. Gene lit another of his cigarettes, Caryl feeling his need to speak pressing behind the silence.

"What was it like growing up with your Mum and Dad?" he asked at last. "I mean, what was their relationship like?"

"They were a lot older than other parents," she shrugged. "My friends' parents. They seemed older, too. In their ways; their mannerisms. In their attitudes and values. It was…cloying growing up around them, I suppose." Caryl chewed her lower lip. "I think I can probably count the number of times I've seen them kiss, or hold hands, or show any kind of affection to the other, on the fingers of one hand." She held a hand up and wriggled her fingers at him.

"I think they love each other. They're just set in their ways, that's all. It's how they function."

"It's a tired, worn-out love." A humourless laugh twisted in her throat. "I've never wanted what they've got. It's like them being together, they've lost something – a spark; an integral part of themselves." She tilted her head toward the sun. "Anyway, I don't know how they are, despite growing up around them. I think a lot has been concealed from me, I really do."

"You think they're unhappy?"

"I think they have an idea of love, but they've never really experienced it. Don't think they ever got there."

A gust of wind caused the willows in the gardens to shake, to sigh. It reminded her of that dream with the trees.

"I think of Huw and Siân a lot," she whispered. "What they had was special, you know?" She threw him a tentative glance. "Do you think a love like that can be… difficult for others? I mean, can it be too much to live up to? To hope for; to wish for themselves?"

"Huw was taken from Siân so young…"

"But at least they got to experience it, even if it was fleeting. No one can take that away from them."

She unconsciously rubbed her scars again.

"Why do you hurt yourself?" he asked.

She stiffened slightly. "I'm never at peace." She swiftly pulled up her sleeves, feeling uncomfortable, exposed. "There's a war waging inside me. But at least out here there's purpose; a reason to be."

She clasped her hands together, expelled a ragged sigh. "When I was younger," she said, "I thought I could cut and see the thing inside. See it all shine out, radiant and true. But there was only ever pain... Albeit a different pain to what I was used to. It became something to focus on, helping me to forget all about the fear I was feeling."

She was about to mention Jake and how he liked to cut himself, too. How sometimes they did it together – our little battle scars, he'd call them. The ritual brought them close, although it pushed the rest of the world far, far away.

Gene stared into her face, his eyes steel-grey and distant. "I often wonder what I can do to see you smile." His brow furrowed. "You smile in my dreams, Caryl."

She leaned toward him, digging him playfully in the ribs. "You think you can save me, right? Is that what this is about?"

He gripped his knees, shook his head. "Don't make me into something I'm not." Then, after thinking it through: "I'm just trying to help. I do love you, you know."

"My knight in shining armour." She sucked in a deep breath, puffed out her cheeks, then exhaled. "My anxiety's through the roof. My flight or fight kicks in over the stupidest of fucking things."

He reached into his coat pocket, the muscles in his face twitching. Again, it felt like he was building up to something. Then the muscles relaxed, his fingers withdrew, the hand unclenched and empty.

Her headache was clearing, she was beginning to feel better. They retired to the hotel and grabbed a snack in the restaurant before the evening rush. Then, lounging on a sofa in the conservatory, they watched the sun go down behind the gardens.

"Remember," Gene said. "If you're not up for…"

"I'm fine, really."

They went to their room to pack Siân's things in Caryl's rucksack. Caryl drifted to the window, gazed out at the bright full moon.

Her skin tingled, the small hairs on her arms stood on end.

She could harvest so much tonight.

***

Excerpts from the diary of Pte Huw Price: -

9th June 1916

I think we will be moving soon, to the neighbourhood of St. Pol, for further training.

I am no longer so frightened. Just numb, I suppose; taking each day as it comes. Not looking back. Not looking forward, either. I am still having anxiety attacks, which wake me up at night and leave me sleep deprived and low.

I am sure we will be together soon, Siân. When we are reunited, I shall look back on this with such relief. That I am me; not this wreck of a so-called soldier.

28th June 1916

Sorry for the lengthy silence, my love, but I have had little writing time and am weary and footsore from marching. We are digging trenches again and making practice attacks, preparing ourselves for battle. We are moving further south to the Somme valley in the next day or so, to join II Corps. Fear is everywhere – in the eyes of the boys and in the faces of our enemy, too. I feel it most in quiet, reflective moments, when I am tired and alone with far too much time on my hands.

5th July 1916

Another quick note as things are speeding up, moving to an end… We have received our orders for attacking the German Second Line along the Bazentin Ridge to the north of Mametz Wood. My heart is banging like a drum! The wood is flanked on both sides by trenches that are held by the enemy, elements of the German Lehr Infantry Regiment and 163rd Infantry Regiment.

Siân – I wish my dreams were as lucid and vivid as they were when I first arrived. What I would give to see or hear you again, even in dream.

6th July 1916

Brigadier-General Evans and Lieutenant Colonel ap Rhys Pryce are conducting a reconnaissance this morning of the ground over which the 115th Brigade will advance. We have already been told that Mametz Wood is "very dense, with thick undergrowth" and "movement for infantry not easy" – not helped by the heavy shelling, which has uprooted trees and made advancement trickier. Bullets and shrapnel burst overhead with frightening regularity and a shell claimed two NCOs in the early hours of this morning. I try not to think about it, immersing myself in whatever work I can find.

I look into the eyes of the other men and see my own fear and aloneness reflected at me. It is this inescapable feeling of abandonment and loneliness amid a crowd that is, for me, the essence of the dark night of the soul.

I dreamed last night for the first time in a while. We were camped close to Mametz Wood, preparing for battle. Hughes was beside me, and as we got talking he suddenly became the German soldier that I had killed near Festubert. I felt a surge of emotion and wanted to offload to him how sorry I was, that I had not stopped thinking about him since it happened, when this enormous shadow descended…

Something was moving through the wood at terrific speed. I cannot explain it; it was like the past, present and future converging to form an absence, a void. Trees splintered and snapped, branches spinning off in all directions as soldiers screamed and scrabbled for purchase, clinging to rocks and trees for dear life.

I grabbed hold of a rock but felt myself shake and slide inexorably toward it. I knew it would take us all; suddenly, it felt easier to let go. To surrender myself and let it have its way with me. That was when this dreadful sense of hopelessness descended and as I looked around I saw that I was alone. All the soldiers had gone. Then the void rushed forward and consumed me utterly, and I gasped awake, my heart hammering, my body coated in cold clammy sweat.

Chapter V

Under the silvery moon, over a shadow-strewn field, Caryl marched with determination etched across her face. Gene was barely managing to keep up behind.

She walked with conviction, with purpose, charged with energy and intent, ready to turn back the days, the years, decades. She'd never felt so powerful. Past, present and future would converge – she'd tear down walls of space and time to find him.

Two hundred yards from the wood, she shrugged off her bag and opened it, putting the contents on the ground. She set the last item down, threw her head back and stared at the bright full moon. Light filled her eyes, her head, her thoughts. She was no longer aware of Gene; only the energy flowing through her body, her veins. "You are universal and constant," she sighed. "In the dark of night, You shine down upon me and bathe me in Your light and love."

Everything was folding, spinning and changing. New shapes formed as the present rapidly crumbled. Gene was cut adrift, lost to her. Cryptic words spilled from her mouth, drawing down the moon and reawakening battle...

Cordite and gas invaded her nostrils; so too the stench of stagnant water, decayed sandbags and rot.

238

The earth was littered with bodies, some bandaged, some splintered, some motionless. Caryl saw blurred movement – soldiers – darting, leaping and dodging through the thick smog ahead. A shell exploded; the dull chatter of machine gun fire could be heard. She found her feet and ran, knowing time was against her, the opportunity shrinking fast.

The blasted stumps of trees smouldered, flames licking about them. Ahead, a mound of writhing figures was burrowing into the ground to shelter from gunfire. Bullets flew but didn't land; she wasn't solid, wasn't quite corporeal. Glancing down, she noticed a boy – must have been in his teens – by her feet, eyes open, lips trembling, the top of his head completely missing. She watched in horror as his eyes clouded; then, moments later, he was gone – whisked away from the filth, mud and shit of the battlefield.

She resumed her search, her heart thumping like a wild animal trying to escape her chest. She noticed amongst a tide of bodies a figure in a shell-hole, breathing hard and fast, spread out on the ground with his hands clasped around his middle. It was almost as though he was trying to say something, but all that escaped his lips were little grunts, gasps and sighs.

She approached hesitantly, bullets whistling, shrieking around her. Then, refocusing her gaze, concentrating, she recognised him – the same face as the one in Nan's photographs; the very person she'd been searching for…

Something warm and bright blossomed inside her.

He looked up, his features splattered with mud and gore. His tunic was torn, ripped and drenched in blood.

See me, she willed. Look. Notice. See me!

Their gazes locked, his eyes widened; then, trying to sit up, a strange expression rippled his face: one of surprise, bewilderment and – yes! – recognition...

In that moment, she knew he could see her, he knew she was there.

She crawled into the shell-hole with him, taking one of his hands, squeezing it hard. She was solid now. Real. Beneath the sliminess of the mud, she felt his callused fingers close.

Another shell thudded close by. Caryl didn't blink.

"Siân? Siân... that really you?" A cracked sob escaped him. "I knew you'd come. But... how?" He laughed weakly, coughing blood.

Caryl wiped tears from her cheeks. "No," she said, shaking her head, "not Siân. Caryl. Your granddaughter."

His fingers were tight – vice-like – around hers, like he never wanted to let go. She couldn't believe she was holding him like this.

The bodies of soldiers flickered around her, skipping and sinking like loose television images.

"I wanted to come and sit with you," she explained. "Didn't want you to be alone. Siân

240

didn't; she tried to find you, see. She… she wanted to be here. She did all she could, then I took it upon myself to finish her work."

His smile silenced her – a bright, wide, genuine smile. It carried none of the melancholy from the photographs.

"You're beautiful," he whispered.

His fingers pressed and twisted around hers, then she cradled and nestled his head in the crook of her arm.

Something hit her then, hard, in the chest and everything spun and wheeled in sickeningly breakneck fashion. She involuntarily let go his hand as he let out one last gasp. The screaming, shouting and machine gun chatter shrank away – suddenly, deathly silence reigned.

Her own ragged breathing punctuated the silence. Panic engulfed her, her entire body felt like it was on fire.

She clasped a hand to her chest, brought it away again. Saw her whole palm was slick with black blood.

Gene kneeled, his eyes large, wild, white. He was with her again, she was back where she was supposed to be and, as he tried to put his arms around her, she screamed; he let go quickly, hands clawing and flexing at his sides.

Something chimed on the ground beside her, catching the light of the moon. A gold ring studded with a diamond and two sapphires. Must have come from his pocket, although he hadn't noticed, hadn't seen it fall.

A grimace twisted his lips. "God, Caryl, what…?"

She spat blood. "Think I got shot."

"I-I'll get help," he gasped, looking around at the night; the fields; Mametz Wood.

As he went to stand, she snatched out, seizing his arm. "I saw him. And in his last moments, I made it bearable, Gene."

She let go.

He stood swiftly, gasping "Back as soon as I can. Promise."

She blinked and turned and gazed at the ring, finally realising what had been on his mind all this time.

***

Excerpt from the diary of Pte Huw Price: -

7th July 1916

Despite it being so dismally cold, grey and wet, the chaps are in fine voice, singing their hearts out to 'Jesus, Lover Of My Soul' to the tune of 'Aberystwyth'. Not even a particularly violent hailstorm could diminish their words.

Lt. Colonel Carden has done his rounds, assuring us that we will take the wood. A smoke screen will conceal our approach, which has alleviated fears a little.

I need to stay calm, need to be an example. There are young boys here, and the fear in their eyes is heart-breaking to behold. Most have never fired a round in combat, and have only used broomsticks, rather than rifles, at drill practice.

We go over in two hours' time. Siân, if the worst does happen, I know that I live on – in you, in Sara. I know that I will endure! Life is precious – we must make the most of every second. Each cherished moment must count!

Do you remember the sandbag I mentioned in a previous entry? Well, when the shells aren't bursting, or the machine guns roaring, I hear it – the sand falling, pattering – like time whispering ever-so-softly away. It fills me with urgency, clouding my heart and thoughts with fear.

I cannot stop thinking about that soldier I killed. If I could turn back time, I would, without a moment's hesitation, put myself in a position where I would not have had to kill that man. I think I die a little every time I think of him. We are the same when it comes down to it, even the men waiting for us now, under the cover of the trees, at the base of this slope. I do not want to kill a single one of them, either.

Siân – if I did come back, what will you think of me? Will you still love me, knowing that I am a killer? That I have deprived a child of his father? I do not know if I deserve to return home and live a life of comfort anyway.

I do not know what I am trying to say here, everything is so sad and wrong, all at the same time. If anything does happen, do not mourn long – live your lives to the full, full in the fullest of God. I want you both to be happy, to know and feel joy again!

Love is the blessed of gifts, and I have been loved. No one can take that away from me. I must make an island for myself and hold onto that love.

Thoughts are whizzing around inside my brain and I can barely rein them in. The truth is, I am most dreadfully scared. I can scarcely hold my pen my hand is shaking so. All sorts of nonsense springs from my mind and the fear is compounded by the fact that you never feature in my dreams anymore. I fear that I have lost you, that I am completely cut adrift.

And that feeling of doom ... well, it never goes away. It seems to strengthen with each passing minute, with every passing second.

I do not want to die out here alone. I am filled with dread by whatever it is that is coming... and it's coming.

It is so close, I can almost touch it.

Chapter VI

Caryl snatched up the ring, then turned and crawled on all fours into the enveloping darkness of the wood. Each time she breathed, pain flared in her ribs, causing her to gasp, to cry out, scream. Branches clawed at her, tearing, snagging her jacket, raking the scarred flesh beneath.

She cast off her rucksack, the contents spilling out across the ground. She rolled onto her back, gazing up at the sky. The moon was a pale, scratched disc behind a tangle of gnarled branches and ivy. She squeezed the ring into her pocket, then closed her eyes and whimpered through clenched teeth, tears flowing down her mud-stained cheeks.

She tried controlling her breathing, but the pain was intense enough to cause her to scream again, her voice sounding unnatural and animalistic in her own ears.

She sat up and shuffled back, twigs and leaves crunching beneath her. She reached a tree and reclined against it, staring through the foliage at the pitch-dark field beyond.

Her vision shimmered, dimmed. Gradually, her thoughts turned inward...

She was a child again, talking to her Nan in Nan's front room. Caryl had her whole life ahead of her and things would be different, she vowed – things would be better this time. She'd seen how it could go wrong and she promised she wouldn't make the same mistakes.

Was she scrying?

Was this a warning from the future?

Nan placed a hand on top of her head, fingers gently caressing her hair.

I discern loops and terrible dark patterns...

Caryl's eyes snapped open.

She gasped loudly, deeply, the pain immense, pulsing through her like fire. Nan was gone and she was here, in the wood, where she'd been all along.

She'd no concept of time – minutes, hours, perhaps even decades might have passed. Shrubs and branches had reopened the scars across her arms; peering down, she saw the leaf-strewn ground black and slick with her blood. It felt as though she'd given herself to this place, a sacrifice for him – the soul she'd come here to comfort. And she'd succeeded, too; she'd found him, completing Nan's work, linking them together again. It was something to hold onto now.

A black wave crashed over her, then voices brought her back to herself, lights dancing, flashing, weaving ahead. French men were conversing in the field, then another voice – a familiar voice – started calling to her.

She tried standing, but the pain was too much, making her shrink, wither and fold. She didn't want to get up anyway; felt so safe in the twisted arms of the trees. They enveloped her like in that dream, pulling her close, holding her tight. Pressing against her trembling flesh like the edges of razorblades. Turning, reaching, she scratched at the bark with her fingernails. Watched blood erupt, trickling down the trunk toward the roots.

Gene kept calling, over and over. Caryl couldn't respond, couldn't reply. That black wave was returning, promising to wipe her out and take her away for good. Like Gene had said, perhaps it wasn't anything to be frightened of.

Twigs snapped and bushes rustled. The gruff voices grew louder, and more urgent. Caryl shuddered as a group of shadowy figures clustered near. It was getting cold, so very cold. Darkness was beginning to swallow everything.

A flashlight beam found her face; she breathed out her last and smiled.

Meet The Authors

Diane Arrelle has more than 350 short stories published and two short story collections: Just A Drop In The Cup and Seasons On The Dark Side. She, her sane husband and insane cat live on the edge of the New Jersey (USA) Pine Barrens (home of the Jersey Devil).

www.arrellewrites.com   FaceBook: Diane Arrelle

Paul Edwards is a life-long horror fan and writes his own twisted tales in any spare time that he can grab. He has seen three collections of stories published – Now That I've Lost You (Screaming Dreams), Black Mirrors (Rainfall Books) and Night Voices (Demain Publishing), the latter being a joint-collection with author Frank Duffy. Paul is also a fan of role-playing games, rock music and rough Somerset cider.

Karl Melton writes horror stories for kids and adults alike. His tales often involve the outdoors, childhood adventures, finding inner strength, and supernatural forces that dwell in dark and remote settings.

Karl has been featured in several publications, including The NoSleep Podcast, Mother Ghost's Grimm: Vol. 2, and four different volumes of Scare Street's Night Terrors Series.

As a child, Karl devoured all R.L. Stine's Goosebumps series. Now he wants to write stories that will make the next generation fall in love with the horror genre.

He currently lives in Alamogordo, New Mexico with his boyfriend John.

Sandra Stephens is a writer living in the Pacific Northwest with her husband and chocolate Labrador, Jake. She has published several shorts in the horror genre, and while she doesn't always write horror, she likes to imagine the most horrific turn of events in any circumstance, making her an excellent dinner party conversationalist.

Philip J. Thomas is an author and screenwriter from the suburbs of Philadelphia. He is a member of the "International Association of Professional Writers & Editors" and is the co-host of "What Are You Afraid Of?" a weekly horror and paranormal show that airs on Para-X radio on Friday evenings at 9:00 pm. He is featured in Monsterthology 2 collection, released in October 2019 by Zombie Works Publications, with his story, Tinfoil Bullet. His short story, Teddy Bear Kill! Kill! is featured in the anthology, Nightside: Tales of Outré Noir, released by Close to the Bone Publishing on October 30, 2020. His short story collection, Dinner, Drinks, and Ectoplasm, is available now for FREE through various outlets, including his website at www.philthomas.net. His debut novel,

The Poe Predicament, will be published by Foundations Books on October 4, 2021. You can email him at extraordinary117@gmail.com. Follow him on Twitter at philthomas@filmauthor1 and Facebook at facebook.com/phil.thomas.50115

SJ Townend hopes that her stories take the reader on a journey to often a dark place and only sometimes back again.

SJ won the Secret Attic short story contest (Spring 2020), has had fiction published with Sledgehammer Lit Mag, Hash Journal, Ghost Orchid Press, Bandit Fiction, Black Hare Press, Black Petals Horror Magazine, Ellipsis Zine, Gravely Unusual, Gravestone Press, Holy Flea, Horla Horror, and was long listed for the Women on Writing non-fiction contest in 2020.

She has also written and self-published two dark mystery novels, both of which are available to purchase on Amazon: (Tabitha Fox Never Knocks, Twenty-Seven and the Unkindness of Crows).

Follow her on Twitter: @SJTownend